A Mad World

Dante Jones

Acknowledgement

I want to acknowledge the light at the end of my tunnel God. With you all things are possible, Thank you.

Dedication

I delicate this book to all the people who live on the Hill and in the surrounding neighborhoods.

Contents

Acknowledgement..iii

Dedication iv

Last Night 1

The Strip Club 17

Eddies...25

Kayla..35

The Morning 59

The Afternoon..77

Black's Adventure 97

KEISHA 105

Time 119

The Night...127

Purgatory...141

Wake Up 157

Devan and Aliyah 163

Grandmas House 187

All the Time in the World 197

The Beginning of the End 215

Deon World 229

Lowell World 239

Fats 247

Leaving Work 253

Redemption 259

Last Night

Damion never tried to pretend to know a lot about the world in his young life, but he did know this, there was more to her underneath her surface. This is his story. It was February, and winter was slowly coming to a standstill. Along with his family: Fats his best friend, his cousin Deon, his friends Lowell, Keisha and his sister Amina, were sitting on their front porch telling stories to convince themselves that somehow, they were better than the other. They all had desires that inspire them to heights above their current conditions.

Darkness filled the sky, but they were feeling the warm embrace of Mother Nature. Where is the moon? Damion wondered. It seemed to have faded into the heavens that night.

"I'm thirsty," Damion said and stood up. "I'll be right back."

"Bring me back something to drink!" Deon yelled.

"Come and get it yourself, do I look like your maid."

He turns and hesitate for a second. He thought, *did I just see something out the corner of my eye?* He mumble and started shaking his head as he walk toward the kitchen; He thought to himself, *I must be seeing things.* He grabbed two water bottles from the refrigerator and noticed wet footprints on the floor. He begins to follow the pattern up the wall.

"What the fuck, I must be tired." Damion started walking towards the front door, when he hears this creepy sound coming from the bedroom. It sounded like one of the bedroom doors was slowly opening and the hinges needed to be oiled. He turned back and took two steps towards the bedroom.

"Devon are you up?" He yelled. There was no response. Nothing but dead silence filled the air. That is until this ominous feeling came over him. He begin to observe a form of darkness spilling out of the room. It stopped him right there in his tracks—I'd seen this movie before."

He ran out the apartment so fast that he dropped the water bottles. He walked up the steps and pushed the door open. "I just seen some creepy as—"

He was interrupted by dead silence. He started talking to himself as he looked around.

"Shit, I thought it was creepy in there, but it is creepier out here. Where in the hell did everyone go? Oh, okay I see they got jokes."

Damion started to grin, but it quickly faded when he witness each streetlight disappearing one after the other. Just like that Damion was alone surrounded in complete darkness. "Damn, what happen to the lights?" He slowly started to back step. Damion hears a faint sound and begins to look around. He hears it again. Hesitantly with a soft voice Damion says.

"Who is that? Who is out there?" He notice the sound is coming from the stairwell. As he steadily approach the stairwell. It started to sound like someone was calling his name. Soon as he reach the top of the steps. He see Fats lying at the bottom of the stairwell. He rushes to his aid.

"What happened?" He yells while grabbing Fats arm. Damion looks down and notice the pool of blood under him. Frantically asking what happened. While trying to turn Fats over, he notice two figures in dark hoods approaching them. Frantically he yells. "Fats get up!" He finally turns him over and tries to pull him up. However, the oddest thing happened in the process. Damion begins to slip and loses his grip and falls back to the steps. He briefly looks up and see the two hooded men approaching rapidly. He stands up and looks back at Fats, but he is in shock, because it wasn't Fats anymore. It was Damion staring at himself. Lying there on the steps, his eyes begin to turn completely white. He spoke these words. "Death will always follow you Uriel." Damion tries to run but falls and hurts himself badly after the Damion doppelgänger grabs his leg. He yells an agony, but it doesn't stop him from getting up those steps.

With adrenaline pumping through his veins he notices his hands are cover in blood. After slipping and falling again he drops his keys at the door. Yelling in agony he picks them up. A horrid sound is vastly approaching him from behind. He looks back at the main door, still fumbling with his keys he drops them again. He bends down to pick them up. Simultaneously the door in front of him opens. He looks up. "What the—the darkness overwhelms him. Not even a yell escape, as he is snatch inside before the door slams.

Damion awakes in a cold sweat yelling.

"Shit, it was just a dream." He begins to feel and touch himself to make sure he is okay. Seconds, later Damion mother begins to yell from her room.

"Say shit one more time. Say it, just say it one more time and see if I don't come in there and knock the shit out of you. Take your ass back to sleep boy." He can still hear her talking faintly through the thin walls.

"All that damn noise. Knowing I have to get up in the morning. As tired as I am you in there playing

Nightmare on Elm Street. Fuck a Freddie, you better be scared more of me." Damion takes a deep sigh;

"I cannot wait until I get out of here." She yells and laugh.

"Move where? Where do you think you're moving too? With your no money having ass." He just sat there with his eyes piercing her soul through the walls. He pulls the covers over his head roughly. He thought to himself, *now she is a mind reader. Let me take my ass to bed.* He looks at the radio clock to see what time it is. Shortly afterwards he was counting sheep and fast to sleep.

Well this story begins like any other typical story. The year was 1990. In addition, it was Damion, aka D was last ride at Eastern high school, and his plan was for him to go out unlike no other. It was 7:00 am Friday morning, and the sunlight gently crept across his sheets. As it slowly reaches his face, he hears music playing in the background. It's his alarm clock going off. It is playing Mad World by Tears for Fears. He begins to yarn, and stretch, as he thought to himself: *that is strange, I thought I left it on 95.5 FM.* Must have been one of those badass sisters of mine playing with it again.

He laid there snug up in his blankets and begins to reminisce about what happen to him the previous night. It started out a little crazy. However, it turned out to be better than expected. He pause for a second because he couldn't shake this feeling of familiarity when he begin thinking about it.

It was Fats, Damion and Lowell riding shotgun, they were out that night trying to get into something as they often did. Some good, some bad…usually bad. Yet this night, it was a little different. Let's just say it was educational to say the least.

Fats was the driver that night. Who was Damion best friend. They have been best friends since he was ten years old and have been fighting and arguing ever since. Nevertheless, do not get it twisted, even though they were at each other throats half of the time. Damion would have taken a bullet for his brother. That is how strong their bond was. *That is what best friends do sometimes*, Damion thought. Naturally he would never tell him any of this to his face. Fats is a highly intelligent brother.

He is a business major in his first year at Howard University, who also sold drugs on the side. Honestly, who is perfect? Back then, who wasn't slanging dope in the hood. Besides Damion of course, it was like second nature to many black kids. Who can blame them for this shit they did during the Regan-omics years with that trickle-down affect bullshit? The only way to come up was to slang crack. Getting that fast money which led to fast cars and easy women. In their world, it was considered the American dream.

Hell, that was the vision in every deprived ghetto, it was ride or die and there was a lot of dying.

That was the neighborhood where they live, it was called the Hill. With the surrounding neighborhoods being just as bad. It was like this on every black poverty stricken and violent street. However, Damion often thought, his was worse. Sometimes late at night you could hear the screams and the horrid that lurked in the corners on those cold dark nights. Some things are far worse than dying around here.

Not knowing what life had to offer, he thought at that time it was the best thing ever, because that was the only life we knew. In addition, some of them thrived in it like his man Lowell. Now Lowell was a laidback type of dude. His thing was, let's just relax and enjoy this thing called life and everything will take care of itself. However, if you came at him the wrong way that was your ass because he was down for whatever.

Honestly, you can say this about him; he is one of the loyalist dudes you will ever know. Loyalty over everything meant everything to him—that was his creed. He was a little older than they were, also he was the one with the North Carolina connect. All that money and he was still living here in this dump of a neighborhood. Damion guess that kind of thinking was beyond his grasp. On top of that, he was still working a nine to five. He always proclaimed to them that having a good job will keep from falling prey to the bullshit out here like the police and IRS. He was smart like that always thinking two steps ahead.

Mind you, they were riding around in Northeast DC, looking for something to get into. Damion thought it was painfully quiet, like you had better not ask for anything in the store quiet. I mean nothing was going on. Seemed like they were driving in circles. When Lowell says.   "Hey, let's hit the spot."

"What spot?" Damion ask.

"Cool, sounds like a winner to me." Fats replies to Lowell.

"What spot, and what will work?" Damion ask repeatedly. With an eager look on his face, he just stared at them both. Fats looks at him.

"Man, just chill back there we got this. We got something different line up."

"Shit, we should have been doing that from the get-go. Riding around here all night.

You know I have school in the morning."

"They both responded at the same time. "Boy you never go to school."

They both begin to laugh. In a condescending way, Damion started mocking them with a fake laugh of his own.

"Really that's how you come at me? I do go to school—education means a lot to me."

That's when the laughter really got boisterous. Fats looked at Damion for a second and yelled,

"Boy you really think you some kind of ladies' man! That's the only reason why you go."

"And your point is? Matter of fact do not try to change the story, let's get back to what you were talking about. What do you mean by different? Where are we going? Because I hope it's not uptown again, definitely not Fourteen street."

"What's wrong with Fourteen street?"

"Funny, you know what I'm talking about; you're going up there to fuck with those hoes again." Fats looks at Lowell.

"What's up with your boy?"

Lowell started laughing. "You got me." Damion interjects.

"Man, I'm trying to tell you some of those chicks are dudes." I am not fucking with them chicks with dicks. Hands look bigger than mine, keep playing around. You are going to press against something, and it's going to press back, boing. Fuck that not the kid I do not need any boings going on in my life." Lowell starts laughing.

"Man shut your young ass up."

"All I am saying is if you like being poke more than being the poker that's your business. I'm just saying."

They both responded. "Shut up."

"Whatever, like I said, that's when they started interrupting Damion by drowning him out with the radio. Doing the Butt, by EU started playing. Shortly afterwards they all began to repeat the words to the song. Sarcastically Damion kept saying boing when the butt part of the chorus came on. Lowell looks back. Damion started laughing. "Alright man you must admit that shit was funny though." Damion sat back in the seat, and that is when he notice a pad of paper on the back of driver seat. Therefore, he grabs it, and started looking for something to write on.

"Hey Fats, you got something to write with?"

"No but I'm sure they have plenty at your school. You should try it I heard it's a real nice place."

"Everybody wants to be a comedian I see, leave it to the professionals like me. Stick to your day job."

Damion started to look again; he found a crayon and pencil under the seat.

He yells out! "Aye, who maxima is this anyway?"

"Your "mama's.""

"Nah bruh, this that pipe head chic car isn't it. Aye Lowell, you know the one, the one with four gold teeth be giving head on M street for a dime. I think she lives over there on Seventeen street. Suck you long time huh Fats?"

"I do not know whom you are referring too."

"You know damn well who I am referring too. The one they call DB." Lowell answers with a puzzle look on his face. That's it, he yells as he smack his thigh, that's her name Deep Throat Betty."

They burst out laughing except Fats, he was looking at them mad as shit.

"Yeah Betty that's her name."

Fats still in denial, saying he doesn't know whom we are referring too.

"I hear you bruh, I hear you."

He looks at Lowell. "Et tu Lowell, now I'm going to hear this all night." As time went on, Damion was starting to sink into his own world. He didn't know why at times he did that. He was always told it was a Pisces thing. His mind would often take flight, always thinking what he can get outta life. At a young age he knew life could be beautiful. However, within the same breath he knew it could be all gone in one blink. When you are young, you think you have today tomorrow and forever.

However, life rarely works that way. It only gives you brief moments in time. That is why you must cherish every moment as if it is your last. Because sometimes that is what it is, it is your last. Some may say Damion had an old soul and was wise beyond his years. Others may say he was childish and crazy like his mother. Believe me you would pay dearly for those remarks if he heard you. He holds a pencil up and begins to stare at it. As he falls back into the seat and he begins to scribble some words down on the paper. He looks at his work and read it in his head.

> *I was only seventeen trying to cope with stress*
> *With constant mood swings, I am feeling more depress*
> *Always in a corner with fear in my heart*
> *Dreading the shadows, I see in the dark*
> *With visions of terror I dream each night*
> *I keep a weapon close to me clutching it tight*
> *Angered at myself because of my anxiety and fright*
> *Never knowing is there an ending for me in sight*

He always felt when he started to write, everything around him would drown in a sea of silence. Such calmness inspire him to write a plethora of beautiful poems. Unfortunately, he never took it seriously. Encouragement came in many forms; however, he was rarely introduced to it. Additionally, he had issues with letting people get close to even see that side of him. Because that part of him was very private. He practically stayed to himself most of the time. He was a little apprehensive when it came to that. Because he knew he couldn't let these niggas see that side of him; He would be branded as being weak. He would have been a laughingstock Therefore, he kept it in the dark with his other secrets. To him, paper was his world. Whatever he wanted to conceive in it, he did it with a pen. He started writing because he could express himself better on paper.

Damion often remember when the older kids would ridicule him for destroying the "King's" English. Anything over two syllables, he would have made into a new word, it was bad. Therefore, his writing became his sanctuary, speaking was a detriment to him. He hated speaking in public, so he begin to speak very low, mumbling even.

You know how kids are; they can be the cruelest creatures on the face of the planet. You learn to adapt. Therefore, he stayed to himself and became apprehensive, to the point he started living in his own world.

However, as time went on it started not to work. Especially, with the kids in his neighborhood. Some of these kids really needed a fucking hug, or their asses beaten. In the hood, there were three roads to take: get your ass beat constantly; tell jokes all day; or fight back. Joking lead to fighting most of the time anyway.

He wasn't planning to get his ass beat every day. So, that left him with one option, he stayed in trouble like any other kid filled with rage, doubt, no love, and anger. During those troubling times he would just write. Write, write, and more writing. He wrote himself into another time and space. He read what he wrote again, he thought to himself, *it sounds okay I guess, maybe I do not know.* He balled it up and threw it. He just sat there thinking for a minute. Looking at the ball up paper and thought to himself, *I minus well keep it,* so he picked it up and put it in his back pocket.

"Man, where are we going? Hello?" Fats looks backed then turns his attention back to driving.

"Really Lowell, what's up?" He doesn't respond neither. That is when Fats and Damion get into it. In the heat of the argument Fats takes his eyes off the road. In that moment all Damion could see were these bright lights piercing his eyes. An oncoming car veer into their lane.

Damion yells. "Fats watch out!" Fats tried to avoid the collision, but his reflexes was not quick enough, and they hit the front side of the car. Which propelled them in the air. The car came tumbling down in a rollover and kept rolling until it hit another car and exploded. Damion woke up yelling. Fats almost loss control of the car. Fats looks at Lowell then the rear mirror at Damion. Fats start yelling.

"What in the hell is wrong with you."

"I don't know." Damion responded. Lowell and Fats saw that Damion was visibly shaking. Therefore, they dropped it. Damion thought to himself, *what is wrong with me. Somehow, I need to get control of this.* See Damion had dreams, correction he had nightmares that often started out in the form of a dream, then it quickly became twisted. It was always someone he knew that would die around him. These so called dreams, nightmares or hallucinations have been part of him as long as he could remember. Lately his hallucinations have been getting the better of him. So vividly to the point that it's been overwhelming. That's only one part of his secret. Sometimes he would fantasize about them, to the point that he needed it too nourished his soul. Damion would often over analyze his thoughts. He felt sometimes like he was on two separate plains, or existence. He thought to himself, *this cannot be the mind and spirit of a person that is sane. Nevertheless, I am I have to be.* Only thing he knew in his young world was that he didn't want to be like my mother. Some secrets he thought were meant to be taking to your grave.

The Strip Club

Meanwhile, Damion is back to dealing with the two bozos in the front seat. When he noticed the car coming to a complete halt. He starts to look around thinking to himself. *Where in the hell are, we?*

He see a couple of people leaving from out a door, which looks to be some hole in the wall building. Half of the sign was hanging off it. He started hearing music playing, it seemed to be coming from the building.

"What is this, a club or something?"

"You will see when you get in." Lowell answered.

"See what, a doctor standing at the door, giving people tetanus shots as a departing gift."

"Do you ever get serious?" Lowell says looking at Damion.

"Nope, but it's starting to get cold as fuck out here."

"Let's go!" Fats yells out.

So, they preceded to walk toward the entrance. Damion's first step inside was met with an overwhelming scent of sweaty armpits and pussy. It was so bad that it made his eyes watery. However, when I finally opened my eyes, it was like awe, the sky open, and he became one with the universe. He never saw so much tits and ass in his life. They took him to his first strip club. *Damn,* he thought to himself, while a tear role down his cheek.

"Now this is what I am talking about." Damion yells out. After sitting for a while, he did get a little paranoid. He started to think to himself, *isn't someone going to say something to me, I know I do not look my age let alone twenty-one.*

"Hey, Fats aren't they going to card me or something?"

"Just chill and enjoyed the show young buck."

Hell, he just played it off, and kept his butt in his seat, and acted as if he belong. Even though the seats were scratching his back because they were old, ripped, and tattered. He thought to himself, *I am in a good place.* That is when the server came over with two rounds of vodka shots.

"Here's to popping D cherry tonight, may there be many more."

"I'm not drinking to that."

"If you don't pick that glass up."

"What is this?"

"It is called vodka and stop asking questions, just drink it."

"I tell you; peer pressure is a mother." Then drank it.

"Vodka huh, taste more like piss water."

They all burst out in laughter. After taking another shot, Damion vision starts to get a little glossy. When suddenly, Me So Horny by 2 Live Crew starts playing. Everything Damion knew as a young man changed that night. Especially when he saw this beautiful dark skin sister name, Chocolate. She was dressed in a red teddy with ass for days. She started dancing. After a couple of songs and the vodka kicked in, he thought he was in love.

That is when she tells the DJ to slow it down. He puts on Janet Jackson's, *Someday Is Tonight*. She slowly dropped to the floor with her back to the crowd, made those cheeks dance left, right, left, right. She made them bounce off the floor, synchronized to the music. Then she turned around, winked, and would point to someone in the audience, gesturing come here with her finger. It drove the crowd crazy dripping with anticipation. It was as if she was dancing only for me.

"Are you pointing at me baby?" Damion asked as he got up.

"I am coming baby." Fats Looked at Damion then Lowell.

"What the hell...Lo get that fool." Lowell grabbed Damion by his arm and pulls him back to his seat. Damion thought, *if it's up to him he will never leave.* He was like a fat kid in a candy store yelling. "Mine and mine!" He would have hidden in the bathroom if he could.

Damion notice two old guys trying to holla at this stripper. He starts to grin at them. With a shot of vodka in his hand, he turns back toward stage when he heard this voice of a mystical Greek siren.

"Hello, my name is Asia, but my stage name is All That Azz"

In his mind, he was saying oh my damn as he look at her body, and then started talking some smooth as shit as if he was Big Daddy Kane. In reality, he was stuttering, choking and spitting his drink out. He can here Fats and Lowell laughing in the background.

"So, what is your name?" She asks Damion.

"Asia, I mean D." He responded. She starts to grin and begins to rub her finger on the back of my hand. You are cute.

"So, what does the D stand for?" As she looks at his pelvic regent. Every blood cell in his young body must have left his brain unattended because he was feeling lightheaded while his pants was feeling big headed. She leans in and asks him.

"How old are?" All he could manage was an umm. Before he knew it, they were calling her to the stage.

She got up saying goodbye boys. They all replied good-bye. The laughter ensued shortly afterwards again. He look at the both of them with a scowl on my face.

"I am glad to amuse you as always." Fats looks at Lowell.

"I do not appreciate his condensing tone."

"Nor, do I good sir." Lowell replies

"Let us adjourn, so we can go to the bar."

"I concur…off to the bar"

"Whatever, I forgot to laugh." Damion replies

His attention begins to focus back on the attractions in front of me. The females were doing things he never saw before. They were dancing upside down on their heads. The dance moves were like crazy. The things he saw that night he will remember for the rest of my life. However, all good things must end unfortunately. They came back to the table talking about leaving.

"Leaving, how dare you play with me at a time like this?"

Lowell told me, "Some of us have jobs and school in the morning."

Fats laughed.

"You're not ready; you're still wet behind the ears."

"Whatever, leaving here is cruel and unusual punishment."

As they were starting to leave, a stripper came out with the Janet Jackson, Rhythm Nation video outfit on and dancing to the song. It was splits and more splits. He believe she would have given Janet a run for her money. By this time, they had to drag him out of there.

"Umm–what's up fellows?" Damion asked repeatedly as they were walking to the car.

"Where are we going now?"

"And why are we leaving?"

"Come on wet behind the ears, we are out of here."

"You sure know how to ruin a young man's fun."

While they were driving away, Damion stared out the rear window at the whole in the wall club. He thought, *I do not even know its name, bye hole in the wall.* He just sat in the seat thinking, about those dancing cheeks. With the alcohol still in his system and overhype, he begin to talk a mile a minute.

"So, what's on the agenda now?"

"We are about to go get something to eat." Fats Answered

"Then we are going to take your ass home."

"Home! Man, I'm not trying to hear that shit. I am not going home."

"Shit we wasted half of the night driving around; when we could have been there maxing and relaxing."

"Listen to me wet behind the ears, we are going home!"

"And I said stop playing. Where are you going?"

"Eddies first then the house."

Lowell interrupted them. "Yeah I am getting hungry I need to feed this alcohol."

Eddies

We finally arrive at Eddies, after driving around looking for a parking space. Damion just sat there looking through the window after observing the people walking by. Fats and Lowell got out of the car. Fats look back at Damion and starts calling his nick name D. Damion slowly turn his head and look at him. Fats starts to get a little animated with his hands

"See this is how it works you get out of the automobile and go inside the establishment to order your food. "It does not come out here. You have to go inside" I step out of the car.

"Damn, people must be hungry tonight."

"You know how it is," Fats replied.

"Shit its Friday morning though."

As they stood in that long ass line, Damion starts to look at Fats.

"This joint is always pack." Lowell says.

"Oh, don't complain now, you two wanted to come here." Fats says with a condescending voice.

"Whatever man."

"Whatever, you were drooling like shit when I mentioned Eddies."

"Negro please that was them hoes baby." That is when Damion look up and see two girls ahead of them ordering.

"Damn they jive like look alright; I love it when they wear those tight as

Guess jeans."

Fats replies, "It's not like you're going to say anything to them anyway, with your whip ass."

"First of all, I'm not whip, and secondly I wasn't trying to holla at them anyway. He shrugged his shoulders. "Whip shit not the kid."

"I'm not even thinking about her; shorty is on my do not disturb list today anyway."

"I hear you playa, whatever you say." Fats started smacking the air with his hand simulating hitting a girl on the butt, while singing Whip it Baby by the Dazz Band. I looked at him then at Lowell.

"Okay Fats you are absolutely right."

"Aye D don't play; I know your ass." They move a couple steps, Damion looked back at Fats with a confuse look on his face. "What are you talking about?" He repeats the phrase again. With the same expression on his face. The line started moving again and they were next. "Can I order now Fats?" They told Damion what they wanted, so they can step outside and smoke. After ordering their food. Fats and Lowell came back in, talking more bullshit, when Damion interrupts them. "Speaking of bullshit, I forgot to tell you the shit that happened to me today."

That is when the Asian woman who took their order kept yelling number seven Betty, forty! She kept repeating Betty forty number seven. Fats look at Damion, they both took off running at the same time. "You know your fat ass can catch me." Damion yells as they ran around a car. They both tried to catch their breath.

"I knew your ass was up to something with those Betty four teeth. You think you're funny."

"Funny, to what are you referring to sir?" He responds in an annoying way. That is when Lowell comes out yelling are you two going stop playing and come and get this food.

After getting their food, they were about to walk to the car and leave, when they come upon two females arguing, with a dude standing in between them. Damion thoughts were running rapidly, *oh this is about to get good.* All the sudden they begin to swing at each other. They were out there looking like middleweight prizefighters. Dudes fights do not be better than this. They begin to laugh, when they saw this dude keep trying to get in between them both. His efforts where futile. In fact, he was the one who kept getting his head bash in by them both. A moment later, down goes Frazier. The dude instantly crumbles and hits his head on the ground. He just laid there with his arms stretch out in the air. He was in another place and another time. Damion thought to himself, *damn he got knock the fuck out.* As the blood trickle from his unconscious body, the two girls kept on fighting while the crowd kept getting bigger. Blow after blow they fought, they both ended up on someone's car. Even the people driving by almost cause an accident trying to observe the fight.

The fight came to a premature stoppage after the police came on to the scene. Someone in the crowd started yelling out what the fuck is this, no tits. Got damn police they can fuck up a wet dream.

"I know that is the only reason why I was watching, shit." Fats replied.

"I know right, okay let's roll before they start that license and registration bullshit." Lowell told them." "That mess gets old quick." Well you know they all had their issues with the cops for some reason or another.

Being young black and driving will always be an issue. They got into the car and drove off without any problems. When they notice there were more police on M street that were park. Soon as they drove past them, they all jump in their cars. Fats starts to shake his head here we go again. Damion look back out the rear window and saw the cops following them.

"Damn police with their dry asses, you know they are about to fuck with us." Damion says out loud. Shortly after their lights begin to flash, so they pulled over to the side of the road. The police walk to the driver side of the car beaming his flashlight in their eyes.

"License and registration."

"Okay sir." While getting the officer the information he asks him was there something I did officer.

He replied. "Yes, there is something you didn't do. I ask you for license and registration."

"Matter of fact I want each of you to exit the vehicle now and slowly." They started patting them down one by one. The cops begin to talk amongst themselves, until one of them started giving direction, now you can go sit on the curve keep your hands where we can see them and interlock your legs. Damion just sat there with his head hanging low thinking damn, *this is getting old.* I look up and the next thing I knew there were three more police cars started pulling up. They all knew what that meant when they block you in from the back and the front. Damion mumbling to himself.

"Damn they are about to bury our black asses." Again, his thoughts begin racing. By now forty-five minutes, pass and they were still sitting on the curve, while they were searching the car. When they finish searching throughout the car, they ask Fats who car is this registered to son? He told them it was his sister car she let us use it to go get something to eat. Damion started grinning and one of the officers saw him. He started walking towards him and preceded to ask what is so funny then grabbing him by the arm. While still trying to hold his laughter in Damion replied nothing sir.

"Well your night is just beginning boy." Another cop yelled out let them go. You all may leave now. The cop holding my arm begins to chuckle.

"Where do you think you're going? Hold up did anyone check under the seats?" Damion glances at Fats, then lowers his head. Seconds later there is a call coming over the police radio.

"Your ass is lucky," the cop tells Damion after pushing him.

"For now, though because it really doesn't matter. He brushes Damion shoulders. I am more than sure we will get reacquainted. I have more than enough time when it comes to dealing with cockroaches."

They all jumped into their vehicles and drove off. They didn't find anything. They all got up to dust themselves off. They all quietly got into the car. No one said a word, they just sat there even after Fats turn the key in the ignition. The radio was on; you can hear the DJ talking about power. He said to all my listeners never doubt who you are. Never succumb to emptiness, for we all have drown in this lifetime one way or another. However, no one can take your power away from you. There is more to you then you will ever know. He started playing a song; here is a classic Sinnerman by Nina Simone. Everyone remain silent in the ride back until they reach home. Damion was busy thinking to himself, *did that nigga just call me a cockroach?* When Lowell started yelling that was some bullshit. It abruptly ended Damion thoughts. Fats counter that with so what else is new.

"Soon as I drove pass them, I knew they were going to stop us. Man, I'm just glad they didn't' find the gun tape under the seat shit, I just knew they were going to find it." Fats starts looking at Damion.

"You, always with the funny shit."

"Hey, don't let that bother you."

"You need to just be thankful that your but didn't get lock up. Because they would have love you in the joint. They would have been fighting over that large ass." Lowell starts to laugh.

"Do not encourage his dumb ass he will just keep on going." Fats replied

"Lowell, you can laugh man that shit was funny as hell. Picture his fats ass getting chase around the jail cell."

"Funny my ass, that shit isn't funny at all." They just sat in the car for a while just talking shit listening to music and eating. When Damion hears one of his favorite songs on the radio Smooth Operator by Big Daddy Kane playing.

"Hey, turn that joint up," he started repeating the lyrics to the song. When Fats ask, Damion if he wanted something to drink.

"Nah I am straight besides you know I don't drink that piss water."

"Cool, more for us." Fats responded. That is when Lowell started being disrespectful.

"Nobody trying here this bullshit, fuck rap."

"I am about to change the station."

"I need to hear some of that quiet storm type of shit." Damion started looking at Fats. "   "What's up with your boy?"

"Nigga what, fuck rap, so we can listen to some quiet storm shit."

"Nigga did I stutter." Damion looks at Fats again with a confuse look on his face.

"Man, no one up in here is in love" They both look at Damion. Fats yells bullshit. Then Lowell says the lies you tell.

"Yeah whatever there are no females up in here?"

"Are you smoking your own shit again?"

"Smoking what again, keep talking shit."

"Yeah, yeah that is my clue I am out. Let me leave you two lovebirds alone so you can cuddle up tonight looking like a fake ass George and Wheezy out here." As soon as Damion got out of the car Fats yelled out.

"Fuck you."

"No that's what you two are about to do. Holla at your boy in the morning and you can keep the details of this to yourselves."

Kayla

Soon as he walk into the house, he hears his phone ringing. Thinking to himself, *I already know who that is. It is probably Kayla I will call her back later; I am about to jump in the shower.* After getting out the phone started ringing again.

Kayla is Damion girlfriend; they have been seeing each other for about five or six months now. At the time they met, he was just getting over his ex, Eva, who was a tall slim beautiful model who went to Eastern as well. Eva clearly had a *yes* spell on him because he could never say no to her. Until he decided to dump her self-righteous, conceited spoil, stuck up ass. Fucking Geminis, they are the worst.

As you can see, he took their breakup a little hard. He met Kayla around September just before school started up. She was a senior at Coolidge High School. She worked at Kenny's at Hechinger Mall. That is where they met; she caught him staring at her outside the store one night when he was walking by. She waved at him to come into the store. He started to look around because no one on the block bought shoes from Kenny's. You would have gotten your ghetto pass revoke. However, she was fine as hell though.

So, he proceeded to walk into the store.

"How can I help you?" she asked.

"I am looking for some shoes."

"Really? So that's what you were staring at?"

"Umm Yeah."

"Umm hmm, what kind of shoes?"

"I don't know yet, but what do you have?

She proceeded to show him some shoes. So about forty-five minutes later, and still looking, she catches Damion staring at her butt.

"You do not want to buy any shoes, do you? Besides the way you are dressed you do not look like you buy shoes from here anyway."

He smiled. "Okay you got me."

"If you wanted my number, all you had to do was ask."

He walk out of there with number in his hand thinking: *damn, she got to have a boyfriend.*

Fine and built like that. He thought he must be on Fantasy Island. Where all your dreams come true.

Nevertheless, like all relationships there is always going to be some good and some bad he thought. Oh, her mouth was as bad as it could get. And the jealousy, dare he say just a hint of craziness.

Sometimes it comes with the territory. He already knew what she is going to say.

"Finally, my bed, it is time to relax. He felt himself dozing off a little when he was startle by the phone ringing again.

"Shit! I forgot to call her back. Here we go." I answer the phone with hey.

"Hey that's all you have to say is hey, we aren't in kindergarten."

"So, where have you been?"

"Out with the fellas."

"So, when did bitches become fellas?" I looked at my phone and started laughing. "What are you talking about I wasn't with any females I was with Fats and them."

"Oh, you think this is funny I haven't seen or heard from you since earlier today."

"Well I wasn't in the house, and it isn't like l can come and see you because you're on a twenty-four-hour lock down."

"Besides you were at work anyway."

"Keep cracking jokes."

"What, I'm not making any jokes I'm just saying."

"You are just saying what?"

"First, your ass is the reason why I'm on this damn punishment, trying to be with your ass."

Damion starts to get a little flustered.

"Man calm your ass down. I'm not trying to here all that noise you are spitting in my ear right now."

"Calm my ass down."

"Yes, calm your ass down."

"Okay since you want to hang out with the fellas, let me spit these few words to you."

"How about you go fuck them tomorrow then, because you won't get any of this."

"Now, calm that down."

All he heard was a click.

"Hello." *I know she did not just hang up on me.*

He was still talking on the phone as if she was still there.

Oh, you are funny; I know she did not just carry me. Shit I think I handle that all wrong. Hold up, what did she say? I thought to, was she saying what think she was saying. Was I supposed to been getting some tomorrow?

Oh, hell no I am calling her back man I have been trying to hit that for months. No fuck that she just carried me. She will call me back she always does. Ten minutes passed by. He started thinking, *is there something wrong with my phone?* Shit let me check. Okay I hear a dial tone, let me hang up she might be trying to call me now. Hmm the telephone cord is still connected. Another Five minutes pass. Shit still no ring let me check again. Shit I need to stop playing and swallow my pride and call this girl. He grabs the phone and was about to dial when the phone rang. He starts to smile and answer the phone hello. There was nothing but dead silence.

"Kayla, I am sorry for being a jerk you know you mean a lot to me; you are the only one that puts a smile on my face." She finally answers, so why do you act like that?"

"Especially, when you say you love me?"

"I guess I never been in a relationship like this before and I don't know how to handle it." "So why didn't you call me back then?"

"Stupid pride I guess but I was just about to call you my phone was in my hand."

"No, you weren't, why are you lying?"

"Seriously I was. I would never take you for granted, you mean everything thing to me.

"You know you feed my soul; you are my Cancer queen. Kayla responded, and you are my Pisces king." I can hear her laughing.

"You know you can be corny right."

"For you I will be that, I am sorry, I know I mess up." "Can you find it in your heart to forgive me?"

"I can, but don't be sorry just don't let it happen again or you will be."

"Okay I hear you. Now let's talk about tomorrow?"

"What about tomorrow?" My voice begins to crack a little, while trying to talk umm–I mean you were saying something about it. Kayla responds umm–hmm, what are you trying to say?

"You know what I'm trying to say."

"Then say it D."

"Okay earlier were you trying say that we should go all the way?" Kayla answers, I wanted to, but you fuck that all up.

"Come on now, let's not be so hasty. However, if you really do not want too, I will understand, I do not want to put any pressure on you. So, when you are ready just let me know."

"Okay I will think about it; you have a good night."

"Good night baby. I am about to go to sleep I will call you tomorrow."

I started thinking; *damn she is right I fuck that all up. How in the hell did I mess that up?*

Always being his reckless self, he just sat there shaking his head thinking I am not going to be able to get any sleep tonight.

He got up and put some clothes back on to go outside, because he was bored as hell. He see Lowell walking up the steps.

"Hey where Fats at?"

"Oh, he is still in the car he wants to holla at you too. Hey, you gone Lo."

"You know it; I have to get up in a couple of hours to make this money."

"I hear you dog. Holla."

He started walking back down the walkway to see what his fat ass wants. He noticed the car rocking, what in the hell is he doing in there. He moves a little closer, when he noticed the windows were fogged up. He moves in even closer, now he's at the car trying to look inside it. All he see is Fats big ass going up and down. Hold up is that Betty?

Betty see Damion and starts to yell. Fats turn around.

"Get the fuck away from the car!"

He bust out laughing. "I thought you didn't know her!"

He is yelling get away from the car.

"You told me you didn't know her. Isn't that Betty?"

"Who is that Fats?" She screams.

"I know she is not screaming for your fat ass."

He grabs his gun.

"What is your fat ass is going to do?"

"Do not make me ask again," he said as he pointed it at him.

"Oh, you going to do that. Hey, stop playing around. That shit is not funny point that joint somewhere else."

"Oh no nigga everything funny, huh. Laugh now nigga."

He yells holla as he turned around and started walking back to his place. Seeing his fat ass like that was going to leave a mark on my soul for the rest of my life I think I am going to throw up. I get back in the house it's time for me to take my butt to sleep.

Damion eyes were close, but he can feel someone breathing on his face. He open his eyes, and all he can see is these two big eyes staring at staring back at him saying wake up sleepy head. It is his little sister.

"What do you want Maria?"

"You're supposed to take us to school."

"Not today, Devon is going to take you."

"But you promised."

"I know I did, but I will take you tomorrow."

"Okay," she started whispering, "You know Devon is going to be mean to us."

"I will talk to him. I'll make sure he won't be mean to you."

"Okay, you better; because he is really a meanie."

He shook his head and thought, *it is too early for all of this.*

He laid back down. The phone started ringing, but when he reached for it, it stop. It rings again so he pick it up, no answer, just silence. He see his brother, then hangs up the phone.

"A Devon come here. He comes, yes. Hey, cool it with your sisters today when you walked them to school."

"They are always walking so slowly."

"I do not care. Do not let them tell me you been mean to them again; you know they tell it all."

"Okay I have to go. Are you going to school? He looks at his brother and said never mind I already know the answer to that question."

"No one likes a smart ass. Matter of fact, get out of here before you all be late for school."

"Oh, that will never happen, I am never late or have ever miss a day of school."

"Yeah, I know Mr. Perfect attendance can you let me get back in the bed please." He thought he had some time to himself before his mother wakes up. Soon as he get back in the bed the phone, rings again.

"Damn who is this now? Hello."

"Good morning, baby."

"Good morning, Kayla what's up with you? I thought you would be on your way to school by now."

"No, I want to see you today." Damion nearly drops the phone then proceeded to put his sexy voice on.

"Oh really, so what you trying to do girl."

"We will talk about it when I come over."

"Okay that sounds good to me. See you when you get here." He jump up out of the bed yes there is a God. It is going to be on and popping, oh shit wait a minute she cannot come over here. He ran back to the phone, please pick up the phone please pick up the phone. She answers the phone. "Hey, you, are you still there?"

"Yes, what is wrong?"

"I was wondering, I do not think it is a good idea for you to walk all the way over here. How about I walk to your house instead we can hang out there."

"Boy, my mother is home she is off today, so I am coming over there." He hesitated for a second. "Oh, okay I will see you when you get here." He thought, *fuck how I am going to do this*. There was a serious problem at Damion house. There has been an ongoing war raging between the roaches and the mice at his apartment. The roaches are winning they got the numbers. "Furthermore, where are we, going to sit at. The couch looks like it collapsed on itself. It looks like a use furniture shop in here. Besides, my mother is still asleep." He starts to shake his head.

"This is more than embarrassing this is pathetic." Then a bright light went off in his head. His heart starts racing as he dials Fats number.

"I hope he still not acting stupid from last night."

"Hey, Fats what's up, what are you doing today?"

"Who is this?"

"Hey, Fats stop playing."

"Let me say it again, who is this?"

"Hey, Fats stop playing. Damion hear a click I know his fat ass did not just hang up on me. I call again."

"What's up Fats?"

"Who is this?"

"Man, why are you playing? I need a favor."

"You know I am just messing with you. What's up?"

"Hey, Kayla is trying to come over and I am trying to take her up to your place."

"What the hell nah, this is not a motel, click.

"I know he did not just—the next person hang up on me it is on."

Damion calls again. Fats answers.

"Who is this?"

"Aye Fats that is cold man."

"Boy get your panties out your ass and stop crying. You know she is welcomed over here.'

'Thanks man, I appreciate it. You are a true friend, and a fat ass one too, bye.'

I can hear him yelling. Click I hung up on him. Have that taken care of please. Now it is time to get dress. As I walk out the room, I see my sister Amani getting ready for school.

"Hey, what's up?"

"Nothing just getting ready to meet Paula to catch the bus."

Damion sister and their lovely know it all ass cousin, Paula, went to Dunbar high school across town. "

"Tell Paula I said hi." She laughs, yeah whatever. He walks out the door thinking this is going to be my best day ever not realizing it will be the day that will change my life.

He sat on the front steps waiting for his girl thinking it must be sixty-seventy degrees out here today this is some crazy as weather. When he sees Keisha coming out of her building. It was directly across Damion's building. They had an odd relationship; they have been friends since the fourth grade. They used to be best friends until she grew some breast and a butt with her half Black half, I got Indian in my family ass. Then everybody wanted to be her friend. Well that's usually how the story goes.

"Good morning, D. How are you doing?"

"I am okay. How are you doing?"

"I am fine you going to school today?"

"Is that the question of the day?"

"I was just asking because we got a Spanish quiz today. You don't have to sound all salty either."

"Damn what is biting you on your ass today?"

"Not you and those lips of yours, I do not even know why I even bother with you sometimes. You probably out here waiting on that big head ass girl of yours."

"Hey that is her ponytail it makes her head look big."

"Boy whatever, do it look like I care."

"I can't tell, because it's looking like something; you are always up in my business. You don't hear me talking shit to you about those fake as hustlers you be messing with."

"Fake as hustlers. Boy please, you wish you had their money."

"I got money! I do not know what you're talking about."

"Boy, no one is talking about that McDonald's type of money your making."

"Oh, you are fucking hilarious."

By this time, Damion sister walks out the door. Are you two all right? I can hear you all the way back in the house. At the same time, we both say its each other. That is her while she says that is him.

"Hey Keisha."

"Hey Amani, what's up?" Damion looks up and see his girl walking down the street. His sister turns and see her walking towards them. Oh, hell no I am gone you know I cannot stand that bigheaded hoe. Keisha starts laughing I knew that is who you were waiting for. I will talk to you later Keisha. First, she does not have a big head and she looks better than both of you do. Whatever they replied, as they both started walking in opposite directions. Damion gets up; hey, Keisha let me know what happened in class today,

"I am not telling you shit."

"Girl whatever, you know you are so stop playing."

"Boy you are not like that, talk to you later bye."

He turns and see his sister and his girl walking by gritting on each other. Kayla is looking upset, but he was paying more attention to that body of hers. He thought, *have mercy on me.*

"I see your sister still have an eye problem that I need to solve. I do not know what her issue is, but I am the right bitch."

Damion was in a trance as if she was standing there naked.

"D, are you listening to me? What are you staring at?"

"Huh? Oh, nothing. Girl you are a church girl and a catholic one at that. Stop faking no one is trying to hear all that nonsense. Matter of fact where my smile at?" She starts to blush and smile. There it goes as I begin to hug and then kiss her on her cheek.

"Is everything okay?"

"Yeah baby I am fine."

"Well, all right then, I see you rocking the ponytail."

"You know it, is there something wrong with it?"

"Oh, no it is cool. Hey, there is a slight change of plan. We are going up to Fats apartment instead of mine."

"Why Fats place?"

"I thought my mom would be gone by now, but she is still asleep."

"We will be quiet and discreet baby."

I am starting to think; *you really are crazy and freaky. Yes, she is the one.*

"No. Besides, you remember what happened the last time you two met."

"Yeah, you got a point there."

"The only place left is Fats."

"I still do not know though. He always seems to be staring at me."

"Girl that is probably that lazy eye of his. Besides, he has a girlfriend. He loves her, that is all he ever talks about Betty this and Betty that. I be like chill with all that noise; I know you are in love, but damn."

After walking upstairs, he begins to knock on Fats door. There was no answer.

"D, I thought you said he was home."

"He's home. He's just being an ass."

He knock again.

"Who is it?" Fats answered.

"Fats stop playing!"

He opens the door. "Welcome to my home."

"I see you got jokes today."

"I do not have the slightest idea what you are talking about," Fats replied... "You may have a seat. Kayla. Do you want anything to drink?"

"No thank you I am okay."

"Fats, I will take a glass of water," I said.

"I guess you will be getting it yourself too."

"It's like that?"

"Yes, it's like that."

He gets up and walk into the kitchen Fats follows him. They both begin to whisper.

"Why are you being an ass?"

"Oh, you like to play on the phone, do you?"

"You were the one who started this shit last night."

"Hey, what you cooking it smells good?"

"I am cooking some of that "none of your business"." Fats walk out of the kitchen. "Kayla, do you want anything to eat?"

"No thank you, I already had something to eat."

I grab two sausages. "Talking about none of my business. I'll show you, '*none of my businesses.*

Damion walk back to the couch when he noticed Kayla with this strange look on her face. He ask her what's up. She starts moving her mouth without any sound. He slightly turns his head trying to read her lips. She starts cutting her eyes at Fats. He looks at Fats; all he is doing is reading a magazine. Shortly Damion focus is back on the worm inside a bottle of liquor.

"Fats, do people drink this tequila with a worm in it? That sounds like some nasty as shit."

Before Damion can finish talking Kayla starts clearing her throat making a lot of noise. He ask her again what's up. She says oh nothing and starts to nod her head in the direction of Fats again.

He looked back at Fats again. He is still reading his magazine I look back at Kayla, with a blank expression on my face, as to say what is it. She just looks at him.

Damion grab a magazine off the table and start reading it. While he is looking at the magazine, he says aloud, "Hey, Fats Kayla, do not like it when you stare at her it creeps her out." Fats gives Damion an angry glare.

"My bad I wasn't staring I was looking at her head."

"My head what is wrong with my head?"

"Oh, no it is nothing. I thought I saw something."

Damion looks at Fats and puts his middle finger up and mouthed, *you think that shit is funny.*

Soon as Kayla turned her said Damion stop moving his lips.

"I think it is time for us to head to the room."

Kayla gets up and say, "I hope I can meet your girl Betty one day."

I look back at Fats with a slight grin on my face. He sat there looking stupid with a mean as look on his face. She stop him at the door.

"D, that was embarrassing. Why would you say that like that in front of him?" She had her hand covering her face shaking her head. "Something is wrong with you."

"I know, I have no filter. Now get in this room."

She walks into the room and close the door behind them. They both sat on the bed where silence was the only action going on between them. He moves closer and leans in to kiss her. She begins to kiss him back. It is on now she gets on top and starts to kiss him more aggressively. Her breathing becomes more rapid and heavier. Damion tries to rip her clothes off, when she stops him. She starts to whisper in his ear then she gets up he tried to grab her by the hand to pull her back to him. However, she lets his hand go. She begins to walk to the middle of the floor. She stops and stands there for a second. Picture this she was wearing a short one-piece denim skirt outfit with white classic reeboks. She slowly takes hers skirt off and turns around. The color of the day was red. He was hypnotized like a bull staring at a matador's red flag. He finally found out what a thirty-six C cup looks like. The word damn, damn and damn kept running rapid in his head. To him she was built like no other. He thought, *being a cheerleader must have its advantages.*

She starts to walk back slowly and seductively. He begins to throb with anticipation. She stands directly in front of him and turns around and bends over.

Then drops to the floor in a split and asks him if he like what he see.

After his eyes jumped back into his head, he tells her, "Hell yeah."

With her back still facing him, he smack her on the ass. She turns around and helps him take his pants off. She gets on top and straddle him. He begins to lay back, when she leans in closer and kisses his ear. Followed with kisses on his neck and chest. She slowly comes back up to his neck. She rises to take her bra off. He was speechless, his thoughts were speechless. Finally, one thought did get through, *who is this girl.* That's when she lays on his chest and starts to whisper in his ear again. He started laughing, shortly afterwards his laughter begins to fade.

"Stop, hold up, time out. What did you say?" He gets up as Kayla falls to her side.

"What's wrong baby?"

"What did you say again?"A considerable amount of time passes by before they came out the room. They both sat back down on the couch in complete silence. Fats look at them both.

"Is everything okay?"

"Umm–yeah," we both answered.

"I must catch my bus," Kayla said.

Kayla gets up while Damion just sits there, staring into deep space. Fats noticed her staring at him because he was staring at her. Damion comes back to reality when he hears his name being call repeatedly.

Kayla looks at him and ask, "You're not going to walk me to the bus stop?"

"Oh, my fault I didn't hear you."

"I see so what else is new."

"Hold up let me holla at Fats real quick."

They left Fat's house with echoes of dead silence flowing between them. As they approach the bus stop the awkward silence between them was beginning to show its frustration on Kayla's face. Damion takes a deep breath. He was in deep thought, seemingly he was a little caught off guard with the question whispered in his ear. She wanted him to do something for her. At, that time he thought the act had all the wrong D's associated with it. Like disgusting, distasteful and dreadful. She wanted oral sex from him. He thought to himself, *it's funny because it was the second time he was asks to do that.* However unlike the first time he was ask he oblige Kayla. So, he jump headfirst without the slightest idea what he was doing. Flashback of screams pop in his head. *Damn did I bite her? Maybe I should have been more honest with her. Telling her I have an amazing tongue, like a Jacuzzi. More like a tub I'm blowing bubbles in it.*

He thought I know it's 1990 but times hasn't gotten that progressive. No one in the hood is doing that, and if you were, you sure as hell didn't tell anyone. He kept thinking to himself, *if she's not going to bring it up, I know for damn sure I'm not going to talk about it.* He hears his name being called. He thought, *oh no, she is about to bring it up.* However, it was much worst then that. She ask him a question that most men dread to hear. He heard the question like it was in slow motion.

"Do you love me?"

"Huh?"

It felt like a left jab to the throat. He had this blank stare on his face. Thinking to himself, *what you think, I just stuck my face in places I never seen that close and personal before in my life.* So, he answer her, "Yes baby."

Now mine you, Damion have never uttered those words in his life. Just when he thought it was over, here comes the haymaker, five four three two one bang.

"Why do you love me?"

With a grin on his face, he responded with, "Because your shit is da bomb girl."

Instantly she gets offended and angrily proceeded chasing him around the bus stop yelling, "That's not funny!"

He grabs her. As he stare in her eyes, he tells her, "Se buena chica, te amo" (Be cool girl I love you).

She blushes and responds, "Te amo tambien armor. (I love you too, baby).

"You know I am just playing with you. Do you really want to know the reason why?"

"Yes."

"I told you, you have that bomb love girl."

She started to swing at him. He grabs her wrist and turns her around hugging her from behind. While holding her arms, he whispered, "The reason why I love you is because you were the first person in my life to show me what it means, and what it feels like to be love by someone. Outside of a few people in my circle, I never had that in my life. No one ever gave a damn about me, not even my own mother." He recites a poem to her.

"You are my heartbeat.
Give me your hand and close your eyes
Do you feel my heartbeat as it rises?
It beats faster with one thought of you
You are my rib that I cannot lose
I don't want to ever lose this feeling
You're my heartbeat that keeps me dreaming."

"Awe, baby that was beautiful, you are about to make me cry."

As her bus slowly comes up the street, she turns around and gives him the softest kiss, "I love you."

He leans in and lays a gentle kissed on her forehead. "I love you too. Because you got that bomb stuff girl," Damion begins to dance away from her.

Shaking her head, she couldn't help but to laugh. "Boy you are crazy."

Life is good, he thought as he watched her, and the bus, fade away into the daylight.

After releasing a deep sigh, he started walking back down to Fats place, when he noticed Betty walking up the street.

"Hey Betty!"

"Who are you calling Betty? That's not my damn name. You damn kids need to stop calling me that. Matter of fact, let me hold something."

"Hold something, didn't you get enough to hold you last night? Then again it was Fats you might not have gotten enough." Once he got halfway down the street. He yelled out, "Just do like Nancy say: "Say no to drugs."

She begin to go on a latent belligerent tirade, which was quickly being drowned out by someone blasting Rare Essence, *Hey-Buddy Buddy.* Damion gets to the hallway he can clearly hear the music coming from Fats apartment.

The Morning

Damion knocks hard on Fats door. Five minutes passes when he knocks harder. Shortly after he opens the door.

"What took you so long?"

"Do you live here?" As he looks outside his door. "Nope, I do not see your name."

"Ha, ha too funny. What time is it?"

"It is 9:30, why?"

Before I can answer, I see Black coming out the bathroom. Now, Black was the youngest of us. He was a straight up con artist in the making. This fool will lie about everything and will have you believing everything he said was true. That is why he stayed in more fights then any of us. Once they would find out he was lying in one of them money scheme they would try to beat the black off his ass.

And you know why they called him Black right. Let us just say his skin tone was a slight shade of black and purple. Always chasing after some big titie chick with his short as he could be their breast stand. He comes out.

"What up nigga?"

"Shit chilling, why your ass not in school."

"What nigga at least I am going. I am supposed to meet up with this bad as shorty in my class for lunch.

"Damn speaking of lunch I'm hungry as shit".

"Shit you're not full yet."

"Huh? What are you talking about? I haven't eaten all day." He stood there with this dumb as grin on his face. He turns to look at Fats they both begin to laugh. That's when it hit him, "Oh that's fuck up Fats, I knew I shouldn't have told your ass shit", Fats has his hands in air yelling, what did I do. Black looks at Damion and asks. "What the fuck was you thinking? May I have a side of some pussy? Can you put extra mustered and hair on the side please?" More laughter ensued from them both.

Damion started pointing at Black. "I know you aren't talking titie's are us? And fuck your fat ass too. Both of you Negro's are fucking my visions up with your dark asses." "Why do you always have to go there with the color?"

Blacks looks at him as he starts to lick his fingers, "I think I have a hair stuck in my throat." More laughter ensued. "See I'll be wrong if I were to go in on those Good Year tire chicks you like to mess with. Ugly in the face and thick in the waist. You know what my apologies for the black on purple, I mean black on black jokes." "Fuck you D."

By now, they were starting to get under his skin. Damion walks towards the bathroom, when Black says to him on a real note, "Asia was asking about you." He stops dead in his tracks.

"When was this?"

"Like about a week ago."

For a brief second, you could see jovial and agony all wrap in one on his face. She was everything he wanted and desire. But she was a little too much for him to handle. Sometimes everything you want and desire, isn't always the best thing for you. She was so controlling; she always wanted her way with everything. He was so enamored with her; he would always oblige her. And she took advantage of that.

He couldn't take it anymore she drove him crazy. So, he just vanished he stop calling her stop seeing her, he stop everything. Well it was easy to avoid her in school because he never went. She had him in a bad place. Damion had to stop the bleeding at the source his heart.

Well enough of back down memory lane. Damion found himself in the bathroom. "Damn how did I get here?" Oh well he thought, then preceded to mix the toilet water with Fats bath jell, He started taking to himself. "Now that's funny."

"Don't be taking no shit in there either!" Fats yelled.

"Man, I'm not taking a shit in here. If I wanted to take a shit, I'll just go downstairs to my place."

Of course, you know what he was doing. Yup, he was taking a shit. "Damn, where is the toilet paper at." He started looking for it vigorously. "Damn I don't want to hear this nigga mouth, found it." After finally coming out of the bathroom.

He hear Fats talking in a low voice, he walks in the living room and see his favorite cousin Deon on the couch. Deon is good dude, especially if you were in his inner circle. However, he put the letter I in certifiable insane. The light skin brother is about six foot three two hundred and fifty pounds. Always drowning in narcissism, he thought he was God's gift to women. Nevertheless, if you ever cross him, he will gladly introduce you to the devil. He was a reflective charismatic sociopath. Always willing to go to war with anyone. Always packing heat no matter what. His favorite line was pop the trunk and you knew what that meant. Damion always feared his older cousin when they were younger. He was a bully and always pick on him.

One day it all change when they were playing twenty-one tag. Damion was starting to notice a pattern, for some reason Deon would always chase after him and he was one the fastest kids on the block.

Before playing, Damion begins to talk trash to Black and Fats.

"Yeah if he goes after me this time it's on"

"What your ass is going to do?" Fats responds.

"I know right." Black said while giving him a high five.

"I know right, yeah I know you don't know shit. The game started as usual. With Deon chasing Damion. Nevertheless, on that day it was too much for him to bare. They seem like they were running all over DC. With each step pounding the pavement it was like a shockwave of aggravation flowing throughout Damion's body. He was aware of the anger issues seemingly making appearances at times in his family. What he didn't know such rage was often the catalyst, which lead to their mental issues. Having the same rage pumping through their veins something had to give. Damion decided to grab a liquor bottle off the ground and bust it against a wall like they do in the movies and use it as a jagged edge weapon to stab his cousin. But unlike the movies when he did it the hold bottle bust open, so all he was holding was the top and the piece of the bottle neck in his hand. Of course, everyone else thought that shit was funny. Not knowing what to do, and feeling more infuriated, for not being able to stab him. He just threw it at him and started to charge him. Deon turns completely red; he loses it and comes charging right back at Damion.

Everybody jumps in the way to prevent them from causing harm to one another. For a moment Damion was ready to fight to the death. Damion thought after that day he saw a little craziness in him too. And we were tight ever since. The one thing I would say a about Deon his family was everything to him and if you had his back. He'll always have yours.

"What up cuz? Shit, what's popping?"

"Nothing just chilling like usual."

"Isn't your ass supposed to be in school today?"

"Man, I have a cold." He started coughing as he sat down. "I'm going hmm maybe, maybe not."

Deon start to shake his head. "You are a mess. How can someone be so smart and dumb at the same time? I will never know, so what's up with you two knuckle heads? Anyone trying to role to Georgetown with me?"

"Hell yeah, I'm down. Wait, where's Black anyway?"

As Fats starts to get up off the couch he answers, "He went to school where your ass need to be."

"Aren't you supposed to be in school too?"

"Don't worry about me. I'm out of high school. "

Damion notice Fats walking towards his bedroom. So, he ease his butt towards the front door, and ran downstairs. He could hear Fats yelling, "I told your stupid ass don't use my toilet! I don't know where your ass been at."

So, finally after all that, they all get into Deon's Acura Legend by this time it's about 11:30 and Fats is still talking shit.

"Why is your head so damn hard?"

"Damn aright you got it."

As they are turning onto I street, Deon ask, "Isn't that's your girl, D?"

"Who, Keisha? Hell no! We just go to Eastern together."

"Your only friends because she won't give you no ass," Fats said.

"Whatever I get enough ass. I never even tried to holla at her anyway. We were friends since elementary."

"That's because you know you don't have a snowball chance in Miami to get it."

"She is phat as hell though," Deon says

"Damn who is her friend?"

"Nigga do I look like the yellow pages to you, I don't know ask her."

Keisha and her friend see them in the car and walk over towards them.

"Hey everyone, so what are you guys getting into today?"

"Going shopping in Georgetown," Deon said. "Why you want to come?"

"Yes," Keisha friend answered.

"No girl, you know we have a project do tomorrow."

"There isn't any room in here anyway," Damion interjects.

"Why do you always have something to say? I knew you wasn't coming to school today."

"Girl I was too high."

"Whatever, oh I forgot you were messing with that big head girl of yours."

"Hey, I'm not going to say it again her head is not big it only looks like that when it's in a ponytail." Everyone starts to laugh. "I really don't find the humor in this shit." Deon started staring at Keisha friend.

"What's your name?"

"Oh, my bad, this is my girlfriend Lisa.

Deon smiles. "HeyLisa."

"Hey back at you."

They started talking for a minute, Damion decides to get out the car. Keisha walks towards him. He asks her.

"Why you not in school anyway?"

"Unlike some people, only take three classes in the morning, you probably would've had the same schedule if you went to school."

"I know, I just don't like getting up in the morning though."

"Really. Oh, yeah, I almost forgot Mrs. Dipswitch gave you an F for this week assignment. Because you miss the whole week." Damn nigga both Deon and Fats yell out. "Do you ever go to school?" "Hey, I went to school this week I went Monday, just not her class, I hate that class. Every day lavantarse, (stand up) Mr. Williams I'm in the class for only five minutes and I must stand in a corner. Man, I don't want to deal with that shit. Do I look like a got damn puppet? Like people are going to be speaking Spanish like that in the future anyway."

"Boy you crazy you know I took notes, so you can copy them if you want too. Just come over later and get them." "That's cool thanks you always looking out I will holla at you later."

"Okay talk to you later." Damion gets back in the car, before Deon pulls off. Damion yells out I knew you love me girl. Keisha looks back laughing."

Deon asks Fats. "What's up with them fools that tried to rob you the other night?" "I got something for that ass though trust me on that." Fats pulls a nine-millimeter gun out.

I'm going peel each one of those niggas wigs back when I find them"

Deon replies. "Just let me know, I'm down for whatever" Damion started laughing.

"You two aren't going to do jack."

Fats turns around. "You think this shit is funny huh. That's your fucking problem, you never take shit serious you always on some joke time shit. Some fuck niggas roll up on you. Then what, what the fuck is you going to do? Joke your way out of it, laugh that shit off. You keep playing games out here like you don't know what's going on. Just last week six bodies where bag the fuck up, six bodies in six days. What you think your cousin is always going to be around or me. Either your ass is going to be six feet under like the rest of these bitch as niggas out here. Keep thinking this's shit is a game. Every time you turn around a stick-up kid is pointing a gun in your face. Fucking eleven and twelve-year olds. I tried to be tranquil. I tried to broker peace even, but these niggas don't understand that shit. This here is the only peace they understand. So, I go out and talk that peace shit with everyone. And soon as they let their guard down, I give them eternal peace. Two pieces of lead to the back of the dome." Swept up in emotion, Deon responded.

"Nigga that's what I'm fucking talking about." Damion thought to himself, *of course you would*. Fats wasn't finished.

"The fucking police always on our ass, they are either on the take or trying to put you away. Trying to place you in a new residency the morgue or prison. Getting shot up over dumb shit. This shit is real out here, you either kill or be kill its call the survival of the fittest."

"Damn Fats, moms didn't give you a hug this morning did she." Damion moves up a little. "Shit you want a hug."

"This nigga never stops, do he? I see why you two are family you both crazy as fuck." Deon just laughs as he drives. This is all I need as he rubs his gun my peacemaker and breaker.

"Hey, hey watch where you are pointing that shit."

Deon interrupts them. "Hey are you two finish playing around? "

"That's Fats playing with his new girlfriend."

"Speaking of girlfriends, what's this I'm hearing about you eating booty now." Deon and Fats start laughing.

"What the fuck!" Damion eyes begin to pierce the back of Fats skull. Fats holding his hands up in the air, posturing he don't know how he knows. "What, I didn't tell him." Damion imagines the word stupid being tattooed on his forehead. Followed by him choking Fats. *No, this nigga didn't, again* he says to himself.

"So, what you trying to tell me is the pussy god mother is out here telling people shit about me." Whatever nigga he starts to look around in the car I don't know why I even bother telling this nigga anything. Because the whole fucking world is going to know". Just as they were approaching M street. Damion blurts out. "Matter of fact let me out at the Polo store right there." "Hold up we are about to park in the mall and then you can go up in there." Deon parks the car. Damion gets out and hears Fats telling Deon what got his panties in a bunch. Laughter ensued shortly afterward. Which angered him more but kept walking towards the mall.

Barely paying any attention to his surroundings in the Ralph Lauren store. He hears a female voice calling his name DJ, which wakes him up from his walking comatose. He turns around. Thinking to himself, *speak of the devil.*

"Well if it isn't the infamous Asia."

"Hey D how are you doing?"

"I'm fine and yourself?"

"I'm fine too." He thought to himself, *yes you are.* Damn she was wearing a black tight jumper. Looking like she was the cat woman in heels. His voice gets a little high when he tells her she is looking good. He coughs a little too clear his throat. She grins as she steps closer towards him, and slightly looks in his bag. "I remember when you use to buy me things. Do you remember that?" His voice gets high and pitchy. He clears his throat again, umm—yes. She steps even closer she's now in his personal space. "You know I miss us. You don't miss us?" Damion tries to answer but he was tongue-tied. "Umm I mean you alright.

Thinking to himself, use your words D use your words. "You just stop calling and stop coming around. What happened was I too much for you to handle? Was I that much of a bitch?" Before he could answer some big as swollen looking dude coming towards my direction. Do we have a problem? I said, do we have a problem? A confuse Damion looks at Asia. She looks down at the floor with the look of shame and fear upon her face. "What nigga the only problem we're having is your ass need to lay off the steroids veins about to pop out of your forehead in shit?" Asia starts to grin. He looks at her oh you think he's funny. With fear in her voice all we were doing was talking baby. "Don't give me that all we were doing is talking baby shit I know when your skinny ass is flirting and how your ass wiggle when you see a nigga. You think I'm stupid? The only person your ass supposed to be talking to is me. Every time I turn around you are up in some nigga face, he, he, ha, ha, smiling showing all you're got damn teeth and shit." He turns back to Damion and begin to take a step towards him. He takes a step back and before they knew it security rush over and gets in between them. He starts yelling this shit isn't over. Then begins to yell at her you know that's your ass right as they walk down the hallway. She tries to look back at Damion. What the fuck is you looking at as he smacks her in the back of the head.

Agitated to his soul, all he could do was look on in disgust. Thinking to myself, *what just happen?* Man, it's always something. Damion just left he tried not to give Asia and Swollen Neck another thought. He stop and bought himself a coat from the Eddie Bauer. He started walking back to the car. Fats and Deon where already there. Fats was complaining as he often did. "What took you so long?" "Oh, you ready? Hold up let me tell you what happened to me." As they started to pull off, they noticed Asia and Swollen Neck walking to their car. An actuality it was more like pulling her to the car. Deon asks Damion what you want to do. You need me to take care of that fool for you. Nah he's not even worth the trouble. He thought to himself, *I can't have anybody blood on my hands.* As they were passing the car, they witness Swollen Neck cock back and punch her in the face. Followed by a choking session. Fats stop the car Deon and Damion jumps out. Deon opens the car door and starts to pistol whip Swollen Neck inside his car till he was slump over the steering wheel. Damion ask Asia if she was okay. She said yes and thanks him. Fats starts yelling come on man, the flashlights are coming. They both jump back into the car and sped off. Damion started looking out the rear car window thinking, *I don't think cuz even did it to help her he was just itching to beat on somebody.* Still looking out the window He see Asia punching on the Swollen Neck head and kicks him out of the car. He started grinning to himself. It made Damion think of one of my favorite Bugs Bunny cartoons with the baby bunny and the lion how many lumps you want? Swollen Neck got a whole lot of lumps a whole lot of lumps.

"You two trying to get something to eat?" Fats ask. They both answer yeah. They drove to Pizza Hut, in Hechinger Mall. Deon knew one of the girls that work there. That was one of his things he love hook ups. Especially with girls that work in some type of retail store, so he can get free or discounted shit. They were loud and crude as usual while eating their free pizza. When Deon ask Damion "hey don't your girl work at Kenny's?" He looks at him with a slight grimace on his face and answers yes. "You know your ass is lucky." "Oh really, why is that? Please enumerate us." While sipping on his straw Fats blurts oh hell, he's been reading a dictionary again.

"Because I was going to holla at her, and you know what that means. Then Fats told me you were messing with her." With a smirk look on Damion face.

"Yeah whatever you probably tried, and she turned your ass down."

"Nigga please, only thing that's getting turn down is more ass, you know my skill set son."

"What oh I see now so you got the vapors. Get a couple of girls now he's Don Juan."

"Don these, but I must admit shorty is bad though I see you trying to come up. Trying to be like me and shit."

"Hey, my game has always been strong I don't have no worries when it comes to that. Your boy Fats might need some advice though." "Fats, why my sister keep asking about you?" Fats answered you know we cool. "May I interject with yuck, I'm trying to eat over here. Nobody wants you except Betty boobs, with her boobs sagging to ground ass." Damion receives a look from Fats if looks could kill he would be dead at first sight. Besides he already knew he like his cousin. Damion had to clown him though, besides she was crazy too, it runs in the family. He had to point one thing out though didn't she just cut her last boyfriend for trying to cheat on her. Deon interrupts, nah I think she stab with a rusty screwdriver. He had to get some type of shot. Fats said no I heard it was a rusty butter knife that she dips in salt and alcohol and slice his ass with it. "Damn, and she didn't get in trouble?" "No but I don't believe any of those stories. Whatever went down dude knew if he would've made a deal about it, I would have punished his ass." "Hey, you know what Fats good luck with that." They all started laughing. Deon stops suddenly. Hey what you mean by good luck with that. Fats and Damion gets quickly and head for the door. The one thing that will never change is the stories. Everyone always had one to tell in the streets. Damion just sat in the car there thinking about life. Even through all the turmoil we endure there are some days that make you appreciate what you have. Like friends and family sometimes it doesn't get any better than this.

The Afternoon

They finally get back home. Still sitting in the car Damion looks at his clothes that he just bought. Talking aloud to himself. "All white and it's looking nice. I'm going to kill them with this one. Hope it get cold tonight." *In deep thought, wait a minute I need to take these bags up to Fat's place because you know moms is slightly crazy and I don't need her all in my business asking me where's her cut at.*

"Hey Fats, I'm going to take these up to your place for a minute."

"That's cool just put them in my room." Damion puts the bags down on the couch. Trying so desperately to eavesdrop. Fats and Deon where being very secretive about something. They quickly shut up when he walk by to take the bags to the room. When he came back out, he could hear them whispering. He walks by and the quietness resumes. After sitting on the couch, he kept trying to listen. However, his eyes were getting heavy and heavier. He was starting to fade in and out. *Damn I'm tired as shit* he thought to himself. He begins to yarn. All he see is Fats mouth moving saying something. Then the darkness came over him. He slowly open his eyes

"Hey Fats, what time is it?"

"Its 2:00." He notice The Box playing Humpty Dance video by Digital Underground. He begins to yawn, he looks around and see Tyrone, Troy and David sitting at the table, yelling at each other as always. Now these three dudes where the cruddiest people he knew. And that's saying a lot because he's from a place and time where the only friend you have will put a bullet in the back of your head.

Damion thought something was off though. He continues to look around and begins to talk to himself. "Are the pictures upside down?" That's when he notice the fellas at the table, dress in all white. "What the hell" Fats sits down next to him. "Aye Fats was going on?" Fats turns but his eyes were burnt out. He reaches his hand out towards Damion. And tells him he is wanted back. Damion tries to get up and falls to the floor. He wakes up to laughter. He can hear each one of them making fun of him. Damion pounds his fits on the floor in anger and pounces up fiercely. "Shut the fuck up!" The room went silent completely with angered faces. That is until they all broke out in laughter. With a grimace look on his face Damion just sat down looking defeated. He takes a deep sigh and shakes his head. While the laughter got even louder,

Damion sat there soaking and thinking to himself. One of them are going to pay. He looks at Tyrone, Troy or David. *The Marx brothers, if I come after Troy or David the other one is going to come after me. Then there is Tyrone, I'm only surrounded by psychopaths. I don't care how crazy they are. It's not over.*

First let start with Tyrone, he was just release from jail on a technicality. He only did five years on a ten-year bid for attempted murder. Well the story goes like this. Tyrone and his girl were on their way to an outdoor basketball ball game. Once they got to the game, she convinced him to leave his gun behind in the car. She felt the police were out and might be checking for weapons, and she didn't want anything to happen to him. Unbeknown to him was that was all a lie. He was being set up. She could care less what could happen to him because she just found out that he gotten her younger sister pregnant. In consequence she gets her family to pay him a visit. After getting to their seats she tells him that she needs something to drink from the stand. He asks her why she didn't get it then we just came from the stand. I forgot to get some water you finish with your inquisition damn. He just looks at her as she walks away. What the hell is wrong with her, I see she's on some funny shit today. I see I'm going to have to keep my eye on her ass. He shakes his head; these hoes out here are going stop fucking playing with me. She keeps fucking with me it's going to be one less bitch I have to worry about.

A few minutes pass and two guys come and sit on opposite sides of him. The guy on the right ask him, don't I know you? Tyron didn't make a sound he just kept on eating. The guy says, isn't your name is Tyrone? Tyrone pause then keeps on eating. He finally looks at the guy to the left of him. And notice something about his eye.

"Why is one of your eyes bigger than the other, he asks. Big Eye puts his hand in front of his eye. "What, there is nothing wrong with my eye!"

"The hell you say, your eye is fuck up man."

"What!" Big Eye gets extremely agitated. In a blink of an eye Tyrone jumps up and smashes his food in Big Eye face. After impairing his vision. He grabs him by the shoulders and tosses him down the bleachers on top of the people sitting there. He was out cold from hitting his head on one of the bleachers. While turning to the other guy he reaches for his gun. Damn! It dawn on him that he forgot he left it in the car. Tyrone rush the guy as he pulled his weapon out. Tyrone started fighting for it. While they both struggle for control of the gun their momentum carried them both over the bleachers. Once they hit the ground Tyrone pull the gun away from him and started beating him with it. As he got up Tyrone, pull the trigger. However, the gun jammed on him, by this time everyone is yelling gun and trying to get out of the way. While trying to unjam the gun a third guy from the opposite side of the bleachers started shooting at him. Bullets where ricocheting off the bleachers. The guy ended up shooting two innocent bystanders and shooting his own man Big Eye in the eye. Tyrone took cover and hid behind the bleachers until he started running away from the police. While the other guy ended up getting into a shootout with the police. And ended up being shot over twenty times by uniform and undercover police. About six months later the two sisters were found dead a riddled with bullets. The police never found out who did it. Tyrone was methodical in every way. He would make sure you'll never see him coming.

Next the Marx brothers, they might be what you call a little special. Troy and David where always fighting and joking amongst each other about everything. Once it was about who was wearing whose underwear and ended up being a bloody freefall. But if you mess with either one of them you had to deal with the other one. Especially if you mess with Troy, he was a little off any way. Well the story goes like this. Late one night he came home from being out in the streets hustling all day. Troy notices his door is wide open. "What the hell." As draws his weapon. He looks around in the darkness. His thoughts were focus on a strange smell. *What is that smell,* he thought? He stumbles over an object while trying to turn the on light. He slumps backward against the wall. He looks around his apartment with regret for ever turning on the light. It was completely thrash. The object he stumble was his lifeless dog. After noticing burnt marks over his body. He starts walking franticly, repeating no to himself. Their furniture was destroyed, and their clothes where gone. The safe was wide open, and the seventy thousand dollars in it was all gone. He didn't know anything who, how or what.

He hears a loud scream; it was his girl Simone. She fainted after seeing their dog. Later that night he takes her to his brother's safe house Simone argues with him trying to convince him, this was someone close to us. He tells her, fam would never do that to me. "Then what about those other niggas you been running with lately. You know them niggas are mad jealous of you. I be overhearing them talking sometimes. Talking about how much you're stacking. Gucci this Gucci that, them niggas always be clocking every move you make." He starts to think. "You might be right about that shit." He tells her he needs to take care of some business tonight, so don't wait up. Simone slightly rubs her hand on Troy cheek. "What are you going to do baby? Do you know something? Are you going to involve your brother?" "Nah baby girl I don't want to drag them into this. I need to handle this shit on my own." And that he did he slice through them like knife through butter. However, all the answers didn't fit, like the wrong piece to a puzzle box. Which drove him more insane.

A couple of days passes by Troy finally goes to his brother's safe house. He couldn't stop thinking about Simone throughout this ordeal. He gets there and the scene looks reminiscent to the one at his apartment. He draws his weapon. He clutches it tightly while going from room to room. The apartment was empty, Simone is missing. He notices something slightly obscure on the side of the couch. He walks toward the couch and see blood on the carpet, as he kneels, he notice a severed female hand. He loses it after that. I mean he really lost it. His family had to check him in a psychiatric hospital. He was there for a while too. With medication he have gotten better. He talks a little more now, mostly to his brother. It wasn't the medication that cured him. It was the pure unadulterated violent acts that carried him throughout his trials and tribulations. He and his brother David acts of violence were becoming more bizarre. They found out it was Troy girlfriend Simone who set him up. Some dude she was banging had her strung out on coke right under his nose. The two geniuses came up with an ingenious plan. They said they found Simone about a year later in North Carolina living with the same dude that had her stung out. Their bodies were found naked in the backseat of an old beat up 1972 Volvo. Both their throats were cut, and wrists bonded. Simone had a crowbar stuck up her vagina. Also, both of her hands were missing, it was a complete set now. The dude had burnt marks on ninety percent of his body, from a cattle prod. Both of his hands were missing as well. No one seems to know who did it or why it happened. They say it was a drug deal that went bad. Sounds like karma had intertwine with these two.

Now David, the sarcastic asshole of the crew. Nickname the Ice-Cream Man, because he sold a ton of drugs off an ice-cream truck. It was truly a money maker too. It was him and his girl Kendra. He was the driver, while Kendra sold the drugs. She was a math whiz and knew how to run game like no other, besides she flash a beautiful smile and a gorgeous body. Everyone wanted to buy her ice cream. Kendra always had a soft spot for kids and frowned upon anyone selling to them with extreme prejudice. Even so, never judge a book by its cover. She was deadly to say the least, she had to be, to deal with his crazy ass. The money was flowing like Mississippi river. They were inseparable. Everywhere you saw David you saw Kendra. But like all good things it must come to an end. The money started slowly disappearing. They were consuming more than they were making, well Kendra was. Kendra would be out rocking thousand-dollar minks. MCM everything from head to toe. In the history of velour clothing no one ever wore as much as she did. David wasn't feeling it not at all. They would get into arguments over her spending so much money. He didn't like the fact that it would paint a target on their backs. Flash will get your ass killed out here in these streets he kept telling her. But she wouldn't listen. She would always respond with, no one is that crazy to fuck with the Queen B. One night coming from a show at the Capitol Center. She and her sister got rob. They were both rape and strip naked and kill execution style. Two to the back of the head. David eventually caught up with the guys who did it. They were brothers. They say he never did anything to them. He just left them with a warning. Be not deceived; God is not mocked: for whatsoever a man soweth, that shall he also reap. A few days later their whole entire family was wipe off the planet. They were all found with two rounds to the back of their head. There was a cold chill going down Damion spine just thinking about those incidents. He thought, *I'm glad they are on my side.* However, he stayed as far as humanly possible away from those three. He thought, *I might have my issues but I'm not that insane.*

"What are you dudes up too?" David answered you know what it is, we are taking care of business young buck. Damion gets up and walk by the kitchen and notice the pots and the baking soda and all the other bullshit, they just got finished cooking. There sat lying on the table, what looks to be an eighth of a key they were breaking it down. He sat there observing them cutting it into smaller pieces with a razorblade making rocks into fives, tens and twenties. It was crazy what he was witnessing. Observing everyone laughing and having fun with the music blasting. He just kept thinking this was one of those rare days in life when everything seems to go your way. The way you think it supposed to go. He found himself just thinking, *it's crazy how these little things control so many people lives.*

All the sudden his mood change there was an ominous feeling that came over him, it was like nothing he ever felt before in his life. It was like the air around him suddenly got thin. He started panting, it was becoming harder to breathe. Everything around him started moving in slow motion. He notice the bible sitting there open next to the table. Damion didn't know why, but for some reason he couldn't take his eyes off it. Then came the funny eerie feeling, this was the first of many he would encounter throughout his life. You can call it intuitiveness, clairvoyance or divination, all Damion knew was an overwhelming feeling that something terrible was going to happen. Unfortunately, it was all coming to infuriation, he was hit with reality once again, he was reminded how cruel people can truly be.

David stood up and ask is anyone hungry? "I know you're not D." Everyone begins to stare at each other, after a brief delay laughter followed hysterically. Once again, Damion looks at Fats. And once again all he could utter was w-what did I do. Damion just sat there. "W-What, that's all you ever say. It's cool though at least I'm getting some." The group turns on Fats with laughter. I know you hyenas ain't laughing. David answers, nigga what, I get mine every day! "Man no one is talking about those ugly ass football helmet having three plat wearing crack hoe's you be fucking in your Chester molester van." Everyone starts laughing again. Damion sees David grimacing; he raises up out of the chair. "Oh, you think that shit is funny. Troy tells him to sit his punk ass back down. They started arguing, Damion accidentally blurts out. "Oh shit, I didn't know he could speak. The arguing stop and the laughter ensued. That was Damion cue to leave. "I'll holla"

He was halfway downstairs when he notice his mother coming in. "Shit I really don't want to hear her bullshit today. I don't think she saw me." So, he waited there in the hallway for a little while longer. She should be asleep by now. He begins to sing to himself.

He didn't want to go back upstairs and deal with the crazy mess up there. He just sat their floating words in and out of his head. She should be asleep now, he thought as he stood up. After slowly creeping inside his apartment. Too much his surprise, his mother was standing right there behind the door. He thought how she anticipated him coming home at this precise moment. She scared his soul right out of him. He barely had his second foot in the door, before she started to lay in him.

"Something wrong with your tongue you don't know how to speak when you come into my house?"

"Mom I wasn't even all the way in yet."

"That's why none of your friends are allowed to come over here now." Oh, you don't ever have to worry about that! Damion thought to himself.

"Those no home training drug dealing sociopaths, keep coming into my house sitting on my couch and do not speak."

"What do they have to do with this?"

"And I haven't forgot about that big-headed girl of yours either."

"It's her ponytail her head is not that big besides mom you never gave her a chance neither you threw her out when she was just about to say something. And we weren't even in the apartment we were in the hallway!"

Ponytail, funky tail, I don't give a damn! Umm… excuse me, I must be hearing things, I know your ass aren't raising your voice and talking back to me in my house. That is why your ass is on punishment now."

I just stared at her as she gets louder and louder. Who in the hell is you looking at like that?" She starts to rush towards him.

"Are you plotting on me boy" Standing directly in front of Damion. "So, you think you're funny, you big and bad now, smelling your own ass. Try me I'll knock your ass down to size. I'll two piece your ass just like I did your father with his bitch ass. He wasn't shit and you're never going to be anything but shit."

He just look at her. Thinking, *tell me how you really feel.* "I keep trying to tell you I have seen what tomorrow looks like." Damion begins to mumble. "Oh lord not this again." "And it doesn't look bright, with your minimal wage job, five kids having alcoholic living sorry ass. And the bitch who is the daughter of a bitch, who you settle down with we be playing with more balls then the Washington Bullets, with their sorry asses." Damion slightly smiles and thought, *that one was a little funny, I must admit I see where I get my since of humor from.* "Oh, you think this shit is funny huh. I've told you it's the wrong way and the right way and then there's my way." After hearing this for the six thousand five hundred and forty-fifth time Damion just walk away. Saying to himself my future will be better than this bullshit. "And speaking of kids you need to take care of your sisters while I'm at work tonight. One more thing I bet not get another fucking letter this year, about you are missing school again, like the year before. Who in hell have fifty tardiness and fifty absents, what in the hell are you doing or think you're doing in there? Are you on drugs? Keep it up boy, you are on your way to becoming a great fuck up just like your father, not average or good but great. He made fucking up a new art form. It was beautiful and spectacular, and all fuck up that was him, with his lock up ass." He walks into his room he begins to mumble again. "I see why he left he probably got arrested to get away from your crazy ass." Moms answer back in a low voice. "What did you say, keep on talking you're grounded for a month now." "I didn't say anything."

"That's two months." He lets out a small sigh, three months. He just sat there staring at them same damn four walls. Trying to realize what he needed to do and how can he get out of this. Sometimes people think they are the center of the universe and the sun revolves around them. Your way of thinking can be a little obscure. He thought, *I'm sure having me at fourteen was more than challenging. A kid having a kid and ended up having four more will do that to you, I guess.* He flashes back to a peaceful memory when she uses to take him to Spingarn high school with her. He begins to talk himself. Life seem different back then, and he knew it can be hard and cruel especially when raising kid while you're a kid. "She deserves all the credit in the world for going to college and getting a federal job. But damn all that I'm a kid. I didn't ask to be brought into this world. You and the sperm donner did this all by yourselves. I'm too young to be this tire of life, she's driving me fucking crazy." Getting thrown out usually is the best part the week for Damion. He love staying over his family and friends' houses living the good life. He thought any place was better than home. Damion did what he had to do and that was pushing people buttons, he was a natural at it. See one thing about him is, he really didn't care what the aftermath was going to be. That was his creed, he would relish in the moment and suffer the consequences later. He was courageous and stupid all in one. He just set there in plotting mode. By now his mother has fallen asleep, and his sister Amani is coming through the door.

"What are you up too you look like you are plotting something?"

"Who me, nothing just dealing with your crazy mother today. Oh, by the way Big C said to tell you to watch cook and clean after the girls tonight."

"No, she didn't, she probably told you to do it."

"Nope, but you can always wake her up and ask her."

He knew that wasn't going to happen nobody wakes her up. Walking in that room would be like stepping on a mine field. They say she kind of lost it when Damion father left them when he was three. His mother had an emotional breakdown went away for a while. She was later diagnosed with psychological disorder Damion grandmother raise him until his mother appeared out of the blue at their doorstep and took him back. He always believe he received that first eerie feeling that day. He thought the only reason she took him away was to torture him. She always said she was going to beat every living ounce of his father out of him. In life, sometimes the son must pay for his father sins. Something inside her must have died that day. Damion final thought on the situation he really didn't know. However, he did believe they should have kept her ass in that hospital a little longer! That's why they call her Big C. The C is short for crazy just all mess up. It was beginning to show; his family was unraveling at the seam. It was taking its tow on everyone more than they ever knew.

His sister was leaving out to get something from the store, when Damion see his little brother Devon walking in with his two younger sisters. He asks him, how was school? He answer, it was awesome I learned so much today. At this point Damion was tuning Devon out he was going on and on. All his thoughts were on him and how his brother must be fucking adopted, there is no way he's my brother. By this time his sisters are playing in the room. He thought it is time to wake his mother up, from her power nap. So, she can go back to work. Mind you he knew the consequences for waking her up. He wasn't crazy, so he bang against the wall. A minute later the door starts to open slowly. "Who is making all that damn noise in here while I'm trying to sleep?" He leans against the wall to listen. Big C stares at the silence in the air. Answer me damn it! She angrily yells. They both begin to point their fingers at each other. In conclusion she whoop them both for telling on each other. She kept saying over and over I don't like snitching. Hey, He knew it was wrong, but better them to get it then him. He knew he will make it up to them. At this point in time all he was focus on was his plans and the part his mother played in it.

Sometimes in life there is some unexplained events that take place. They are usually rare, but they do exist. It may be so overwhelming it leave you in complete silence. And this was one of those times. Damion observes his mother getting ready to leave for work, when he noticed her picking up a wig off the floor. She proceeds to smack it against the wall and put it on. Damion stood there in complete horror. He believe that the wig was from the kids last Halloween. It look like Michael Jackson, Thriller hairstyle video. He and Devon just stared in shock. His thoughts were on his face, *what in the hell is that on your head.* "What are you two staring at?" Nothing, we both answered. They started acting like they were cleaning. Then came that sweet sound of the door closing behind her. They both look at each other and busted out laughing hysterically for about ten minutes. His sister comes in the front door laughing. "What was that on Big C head?" They all begin to laugh. "Now all she needs is the red jacket and the penny loafers and the glitter glove." More laughter ensued afterwards. "Cause this is a thriller, thriller night." "Oh, my stomach is starting to hurt." Devon slips and fall from laughing so much. Damion looks at his watch. Oh shit, it's about 3:45, it's time to roll. He hears the phone ringing, after answering it there was nothing but complete silence. Damion ponders, and shakes his head and hangs up. He tells them he'll be back in a little bit.

With tears in his eyes from laughing so hard, he goes outside and see three clowns out there taking pictures. So, he joined them, next thing you know everyone was out there taking pics. Fats wanted to run a couple of basketball games. There court wasn't really a basketball court. Being though there was a lack of having a floor. It was made up of dirt. No basketball hoops or strings, just a bucket crape. It was ghetto fabulous, but it was theirs. They were out there playing like they belong in the NBA more like the Negro Bamma Association. But don't tell them that though they were out there taking the game serious.

As always, it begins with the trash talking, then the tension and then everyone going overboard with the joking. The yelling and arguing ensued. Everyone is calling every type of foul like referees. Damion just sat there and watch the game, he thought he was looking to clean to be out there playing.

Black's Adventure

While watching the game Damion kept noticing someone running towards his direction. He kept squinting trying to see who it was. "Hold up is that Black? Why is this fool wearing one shoe?" He begins to walk towards Black. The rest of the fellas didn't even notice him with their NBA aspersions and all.

"What up dog you okay?"

"Yeah man I'm cool."

"You don't look cool. Trying to hold his laughter he ask him is this some new look? Where's your other shoe?"

"This shit isn't funny."

"I'm not laughing, not yet."

"I must tell you about this crazy shit that just happened. You know Lil Eddie, right?"

"Yeah, Mario cousin."

"Man, I told this fool to give me a ride out to New Carrollton by the subway. I knew I shouldn't have asked his punk ass to drive me, but I was press. So, we are driving listening to this bad as Rare Essence tape. When I notice the police were behind us. I tell Lil Eddie hot ass to be cool, because I don't know what he has in his trunk. You know that dude is always trying to sell something hot. You won't believe this shit. Do you know this fool got me out there riding around in a stolen car? Talking about he borrowed it from somebody they left theirs keys in the car running." He tells Black stop playing. "Talking about he left a note on the curved. I saw my life flash before my eyes." Damion is still trying to hold his laughter inside. "I was starting to get a little nervous, when he started talking about outrunning them. I'm like with what this piece of shit Toyota Tercel, man if you don't play it cool. He's telling me, fuck that we out of here. "I'm yelling no! I'm about to grab the wheel when we notice the police getting into the next lane and made a turn at the light. I told your chimpanzee looking ass to be cool, got my heart in my throat. So, we are close to my girl house and I tell him I need to get something from Seven-Eleven. He tells me, man I need a hub cap for the car. A hubcap for a stolen car nigga is you crazy or something. This not even your car, let alone it's a fucking Tercel. Man stay in the car, damn. If you are that press our help you later. I go in the store trying to find what I was looking for when I look outside and see this fool looking at people tires like a fiend. I'm saying to myself I know this dude ain't trying to steal a hubcap in broad daylight. I'm at the soda machine when I notice flashing lights. I see two cop cars pulling up. He tried to outrun them, but they caught his dumb ass. While they were putting cuff on him, I'm thinking I got to get the hell out of here. I walk through the door playing it smooth. I get pass them and started walking a little faster in the opposite direction. I'm thinking, *shit I'm in the clear.* Until this dumb ass stop me dead in my tracks by yelling my name. A Black, a Black they got us man.

"No, that fool didn't call your name."

"Yeah, that fool did. Next thing I hear is the police yelling stop. So, you know I took off." Damion started laughing, well I know they wasn't going to catch your track star ass.

"Two white boys please you know me better than that."

"So how did you lose your shoe then?"

"Wait a minute let me sit down and catch my breath. They look like they are playing for real out there."

"Yeah, they think they got game. So, what happen?"

"I'm about to get to that."

"Did you lost it from running?"

"Nope, so after losing the two bozos, I run over to my girl house and knock on her door, all she was wearing was a I Like Em' Big t-shirt on."

"You know how I do I step inside talking shit, I see you like em' big girl."

"You know I do boy."

"That's what I'm talking about baby."

I started looking around, like damn this is a nice place so who stay here with you. Damion interrupts him.

"Why? Because you were casing the joint."

"Nah, it wasn't like that.

"Yes, it was."

"You're right, I was casing the joint."

Like I was saying, she answers just me and my mom's. She tells me to have a seat she'll be right back. She had the good Luther Vandross, Here and Now on. I see a nice gold bracelet in the couch. So, you know I'm pocketing that. Then I begin to get buck naked. I'm stretch out on the couch like a bitch. D she comes back with a glass of milk and some cookies. I'm like what the fuck. Bitch do you think its snack time and recess or something. She stands in front of me and says I like chocolate in my milk and tells me to stick my dick in the glass of milk. I thought the chick was joking I'm like what. She repeats it again. I want you to stick your dick in my glass of milk. Then I'm going suck the milk off your dick and eat my cookies.

"So, I did what she asks me too."

"No, you didn't dog, for real Black I told your ass stop fucking with those fat bitches."

"So, she's sucking my dick and licking the milk."

"Hold up wasn't that shit getting everywhere?"

"Yeah but she had one of those couches with the plastic on it I guess she can just wipe it right up." She starts to eat the cookies and sucking my dick at the same time. Between the couch sticking to my ass and Cookie Monster grinding those cookies on my shit I don't know which was more painful. Then she drinks some more milk then the shit was all gushy. "What the fuck, man that's some nasty as shit." I told her I had enough of lunch time. So, we go to her bedroom and I bend her over on the bed. I'm hitting it from the back, I mean like I'm trying to kill the pussy. I'm hitting her so hard she and those big as tities where hitting the headboard. Bang, bang, bang, that shit was taking me to another level dog.

She started throwing that ass back, yelling fuck me harder you are making me so hungry.

Damion interrupts the story once again. "Hold up, you do mean horny, don't you? Black looks at him with disbelief. "Hell no, she was talking about food man." Damion starts laughing emphatically.

"My fault man, please continue with your story."

Are you positive or do you need more time to finish laughing at my expense?" As I was saying I was hitting it from the back. When she starts saying wait a minute, you hear something?

"Nope just the headboard."

"No not that silly." She tells me to stop.

"I'm like stop, what."

"I think somebody at the door." I hear a woman's voice. Why is this chain lock on the door? Shelly! Shelly, I know you don't have another boy up in here! I'm going to beat the black off both of your asses. Open this mother fucking door. We both look at each other quickly trying to get dress. She tells me you must go through the patio door, but you must wait a second.

"I will give you a cue. I'm looking at her confuse as shit."

"Bitch do you mean clue?"

"No, a cue."

"A cue, what the fuck is a que?" She shakes her head boy just wait, while I go open the door for mother. I know your ass isn't crazy, where is he?

Where is he? She yells back where is who? There is no one is here mama. I'm hiding in the closet trying to be still. A little time had passes when she comes back and tell me to go out through the patio door. I begin to slowly creep through the house. With each step, it felt as if the whole world could hear me. I get to the living room. Next thing I know her mother pops up out of nowhere yelling I got your ass now, chasing me with a broom. With one swing of the broom she trips me up and I fall. She caught me. Man, she tore my back up with that broom. I finally get up and start running towards the patio door I was almost out of there until she grabs my leg trying to pull me back in, man she was strong. I got your black ass now you're not going nowhere. I'm trying to fight her off she ended up with one of my shoes. I ran till I got to the subway. I get on the train and everybody staring at me like I'm crazy. I can tell and still smell like pussy. Black sniffs himself, shit. Damion no longer could contain himself, he burst into laughter. The laughter quickly dissipated when Keisha sticks her head out of window and ask Damion to come here. He begins to clear his throat.

"What was that?"

"Huh."

"You heard me."

He tells her to give him a second. Black ask what's that about. Beats me, I can't remember the last time I was up there.

"I see your ass aren't laughing now though. I don't know why you're faking; you know you want to run up there now. "

"What please I got real shit to think about and she's not one of them besides I have a girl and we are in a good place right now. You know better than anyone else the shit I went through with Asia, I'm not trying to mess with anyone's head."

"But its Keisha though." "And at the end of the day she has somebody too, you know the type of dudes she messes with anyway. Besides we don't like each other like that anyway."

"You use too."

"We used to be best friends that's it."

"Whatever, I recall there was a story about you two in elementary.

"Whatever you heard was a lifetime ago we both have change since then."

"I hear you talking, talking out the side of your neck."

"Whatever nigga I holla at you later with your one shoe ass."

Keisha

"You know what, I am about to go up here and see what's up. You are going to stop implying shit with me too."

"How are you going to do that still standing here?" He was right Damion was on stuck he couldn't seem move his legs at all.

Finally, he manage to find some courage as he walk upstairs talking to himself. "Nobody has control over my life. I control this shit. I am the king of my world. Not my mother not anyone." He knocks on the door. "I have other things to worry about. I need to be focused on this money. I need to get them new Fila." I knock again damn is she going answer the door. He stood there shaking his thinking.

See, this is the bullshit I keep talking about. She thinks she is like that ask me to come up here and have me waiting.

As he begins to turn, he hears a voice yelling come in the door is open. He walks in and looks around. "Where is she?" He hears the good Junkyard Band playing in the bedroom. He notices some papers on the table. "Oh, that's right, these are the notes from school I forgot about that. See I got myself all work up for nothing fucking with Black one shoe ass. Let me get these papers." He headed back to the front door, yelling thanks for the notes. The music stop playing. "D wait! I'm sorry I just got out of the shower, I have to explain some of it to you first or you will be lost. Damion turns around girl you don't have explain nothing to…oh my damn. He drops the papers all on the floor. He couldn't help himself; he was caught off guard by the outfit she was wearing. She had a halter-top and biker booty shorts on. She starts bending over to help him pick up the papers.

"What did you say?"

"Um–oh nothing. After picking the papers up they walk to the table. She asks him, so where are you going tonight?"

"We supposed to be going to a game at Spingarn."

"Lisa has been begging me to go."

"I do not really want to go for real. I have been having a funny feeling all day. I don't know it's probably all in my head."

"Maybe you shouldn't go then. Maybe your spirit is telling you something. Sometimes when you discard something within your heart it never ends well."

"Sounds like you're speaking from experience?"

"Maybe."

"Okay Mrs. Gloom and Doom, you sound like my grandmother."

"She must be wise beyond her years."

"Yeah, she is or crazy I do not know."

"What you trying to say I am crazy?"

"Oh, nothing like that, you are too intelligent to be crazy."

"Oh, okay good answer; do you want something to drink?"

"No thank you I am straight. So, what's up with this Spanish?" She begins to explain it all to him. "This will be on the new test as well, she tells him. So, what is the real reason why you don't go to school anymore? Because I remember a time you use to get all those scholastic awards in school. You was a nerd, so what happened?"

"Honestly, I just got more handsome and said fuck the books, who needs them. They both started laughing. Seriously, I really don't know, and then again. Then again, I kind of do, it just became boring to me it was the same old routine. Especially the classes I excel in. I would make it even worst. That is how you can go from an A to an F from one semester to the next. School just didn't hold my attention. In the end, I am smart enough to get what I need to pass. It hasn't failed me so far." She grins you think you're some kind genius huh?"

"Cogito ergo sum. I think therefore I am."

"Okay I see you know a little Latin. How about this, as je pense, donc je suis."

"Therefore, you have to say it in French, always the showoff." With a small grin on his face.

"You remember the awards huh."

"Yes, I do why."

"Oh nothing, I remember when you use to rock your two plat ponytails."

"No, I did not."

"Yes, you did in fact there is a picture of you on the wall with that exact hairstyle."

They both laugh again.

"Do you remember the six-grade dance?"

"Of course, I do, you were my knight in shining armor.

"Are we talking about the same dance?"

"Yes silly, why you remember something different."

"Uh…Hell yeah, I remember it differently."

It was the six-grade spring dance. The last dance of the year. The DJ was playing Cool It Now, by New Edition. The pre-teen girls where exhibiting an irrational behavior over that song. I was dancing with my cutie Sabrina. She had the cutest dimples, and that smile. Keisha interrupts me, as she clears her throat. Sitting with her arms folded across her chest. She says with a smirk look on her face, how long are we going to stay on dimples? Oh, my bad as I was saying. Cool It Now was playing, and the only thought I had on my brain while we were dancing. Why are these girls tripping over these guys anyway? They are not all that, they put their pants on one leg at time just like me. As I am singing the words to Cool It Now in my head, Sabrina asks me can I get her something to drink. As I walk over to the refreshment table, I notice Keisha standing in a corner talking and grinning with her friends. Fat Boys Are Back, by The Fat Boys is playing. After picking up two cups of punch, I turn around and guess who is impeding my process, you Keisha.

"Hey D."

"What's up Keisha?"

"Nothing just hanging with my girls. I look over her shoulder and see them still in the corner grinning."

"So why aren't you dancing?"

"Maybe no one has asked me yet."

"Oh, oh really…Give me a second, I will be right back."

I turned around and my progression was impeded once again. As I almost spill the punch. "Hey Sabrina." She looks to the side of me and sees Keisha. "I should have known. Does man best friend always have to tag along everywhere you go?" Keisha grins and walks toward Sabrina. I know you did not just call me a dog. You need to get your girl before I get a hold of her bald head dusty ass. I am in between them as they go back and forth. I see Keisha friends are coming. Before anyone else could intervene, two teachers came over squash it. Therefore, Sabrina says what's it going to be D, her or me?

"What, what do you mean?"

"Just like, I said—your girl or your best friend… pick."

"I am not doing that."

Keisha interjects. "No D, dusty is right."

Sabrina rows her eyes, anyway pick. I look at them both with their arms folded across their chest waiting. U-um I have to use the restroom. I kept it moving until I could not no longer hear them calling my name. I just stood there in the restroom waiting bobbing my head to LL Cool J Radio, when my classmate Antonio walks in. "Hey D why you in here?"

"Restrooms calms my nerves."

"Restrooms calms your nerves, really? Oh, okay, well Keisha said you need to bring your scared punk butt out here or she is going to come in here."

"You know what, I need to let these girls know who the man and stop playing with these girls."

As soon as I walk out the restroom. I feel a slap on the back of my head. It's Keisha, so you are running from me now.

"Girl I am not running from you."

"Girl this girl has a name. We started walking down the hall. What is going on D?"

"You tell me, what was that all about?"

"What was what all about, that girl? I am not thinking her or any other cornball girl you like."

"There you go."

"I am just saying, I thought we were best friends. Or have your training bra-friend corrupted you. I interrupts her, we are best friends and you know that. Nevertheless, that is my girl, so what you want me to do. She took a step back, really. With a scowl on her face and anger in her voice, she says it seems like you already know what to do. I stood there calling her name as she storms off. I look at the ceiling above me and yell women. Ten minutes go by, I go after her. As I walk through the double doors, I notice it was nothing but chaos.

I see Antonio. "Hey, what's going on?" "Its Big Wood, he got a victim. She wouldn't give him a dance.

"Oh yeah," I shook my head, "Damn I feel sorry for her, whoever she is."

He laughs. "It's your girl."

"My girl."

He points and I look. It is Keisha and she is backing away from Big Wood, she still talking trash though. Big Wood stayed back so many times, he should be in the ninth-grade. He was a six-foot two hundred pound monster that terrorize our school.

In addition, it did not matter to him what gender you were, you still received it. I look around for the teachers. There was no insight. I think they took off, because they feared him, too. I see Keisha with this look of uncertainty, vulnerability on her face as she looks at me. She was scared. I thought to myself, *is anyone going to help her.* I turned around and thought to myself, *oh well it was nice knowing her.* Where is Sabrina anyway? Next thing I knew I heard this loud smack, in fact everyone heard it. They were in shock, as they stood there staring at me hitting Big Wood with a chair across his back. Honestly, I don't know how I ended up there standing with that chair in my hand.

He slowly turns around with the smile of the devil on his face. I'm sure everyone there was saying what I was thinking, *oh shit!* He hit me so hard he knock my soul out of my body. Sending sliding across the floor, I had time to reflect on my short life works. Barely conscious I see Big Wood bending over me trying to choke the rest of my life out of me. As I'm fading into black, Keisha runs over from behind and goes Pelé soccer style on his nuts. It took him a second, but he eventually went down. She reaches out for my hand to help me up. But the rest of the kids got between us. Talking about how awesome the fight was. We just stared at each other as we both were escorted away in opposing directions. Keisha looks at Damion, reminiscing of the look that day at the six grade dance.

"What?" He asks her.

"Nothing, just thinking."

"Thinking about what?"

"Nothing boy, as she starts to look at the table."

"Hey, what ever happened to Big Wood?"

"He died from a drug overdose in junior high. I shook my head, that's a damn shame. The black man is an endanger species."

"Let me ask you this Keisha, you think life was easier back then?"

"Maybe, I don't know, but the one thing I do know is I like the fashion and hairstyle a lot better now."

"That is true; it is better."

"I don't know what happening, I guess the world change I don't think we did."

"Yeah you might be right, it just seems like everyday someone is getting taken out of here, in an unnatural way. And what's makes matters worse, we made it all normal. I guess we have gotten to the point that we have become so desensitize. And that which lurks unseen in those cold dark shadows, so desperately wants to be seen now. I guess I will never get it, like this Spanish homework."

"Whatever, I know you probably know this work already you just needed an excuse to hang with me."

"No hablo ingles, hablo espanol un poco."

"Like I said, I knew it."

"Whatever, I don't need an excuse." She gets up and walks to the kitchen. Damn, Damion expresses to himself. He tried not to look at her butt, but it was calling him. He stared at it for a quick second. He was ignorant to the fact that she saw him through the looking mirror. She comes back with a glass of water and a smile on her face.

"Why are you smiling?"

"Oh, nothing just thinking how people portrayed themselves as one thing but are really something else. Why is that?"

"Maybe because the individual doesn't think that people might not like the true version of them self, so they portrayed themselves as something else something more likable. It's kind of sad when you think about it. She sat there with this big smile still on her face.

"You think so."

"You keep smiling like you know something I begin to look around. She asks me so what are you doing for your birthday? I don't know, I'll be doing something though. I was invited to this party so who knows. So, are you going to give me a gift?"

"Maybe if you can act right."

"I don't know about all that, you know that's kind of hard for me."

"Tell me about it."

"Oh, you're funny now."

"Why is it always that I have to act right like you be innocent all the times?"

"I don't know what you are referring too."

Then she tells me. "I forget sometimes how cute you really are."

"Thank you, you are cute too." She pauses and looks at Damion with contempt

"I'm cute. I know I'm cute, I don't need you to validate my cuteness. And I'm not just cute I'm gorgeous baby."

"Oh…okay."

"I have your, oh…okay right here."

"All I was trying to say was—you know what forget it. I'm glad to have the real Keisha back."

"What the hell that's supposed to mean?"

"It means your ass is—"

Before he could finish his sentence, he caught himself and stop. You know what nothing I'm gone. He grabs the papers off the table he stood there looking foolishly at the door trying to unlock it to no avail. The harder he tried the more it piss him off. She calmly walks over and brushes her body across his to unlock the door. Making the hairs on his back stand erect. *Damn I drop the papers again,* he thought to himself. She slowly bends over to pick the papers back up. "I'm not going to keep picking up these papers for you boy. Here boy." She puts them against my chest and steps closer. Damion tries to take a step back, but he was already leaning against the wall next to the door. As she leans in with a smile on her face, she ask him, are you scared of something? He hesitates and tells her no, while she opens the door.

"Goodbye D enjoy the rest of your night."

He looks at the door, oh bye. After exiting her door, he takes a couple of steps and stop because he had to catch his breath. "Damn my heart is pounding like crazy. What in the hell was all of that, what did I just walk myself into? Got damn it she probably was doing all that shit on purpose, fucking with my head. Damn I'm the one normally fucking with people heads. I can't stand her ass. But I'm okay though I think I handle that okay. I need to get out here I need some air. Oh, she's going to pay for that." He begins walking out of her building and see Fats walking up the stairs. Keisha yells out of her window D! Damion gets startle for a second and drop the papers again looking back at Keisha. With a smile on her face, she tells him, you drop something and closes her window. As he pick up the papers, he just kept repeating one of these days one of these fucking days. He finally caches up with Fats.

"Where did everyone go?"

"To take a bath, that's where I'm heading now. Are you coming from Keisha apartment?"

"Yeah why."

"Just asking you were up there for a while."

"Just schoolwork."

"Yeah, I bet. You look shook like you seen a ghost or something."

"More like the wicked witch of Northeast."

"What?"

"Never mind I'll meet you back at your place, alright."

Damion went inside to check up on the girls. Amani was in the kitchen cooking dinner, while Devon was doing his homework. And his mother was at work. Everything was straight at home all he needed was his coat and he was out. Amani call Damion while he was still at the door.

"Yeah what's up?"

"Nothing. Are you leaving now?"

"Yeah, what's up?"

"Nothing just be safe tonight."

"You know me I am what I am."

"That's what I'm afraid of."

"Girl, I'll be okay goodnight."

Time

Damion goes back outside and the first thing he see is Fats, out talking to the fellas.

"I thought you were going in the house."

"Every time I try to get out the game, they pull me back in. Always trying to take my throne."

"You know I can't let that happen."

"Apparently not, I see. I'll give to Fats; he can play some ball even on the real courts. You can hear him yelling time out, oh now he wants to come out of the game."

"What you tire now? Trying to catch his breath he tells him hell no I'm okay."

"Then why does it look like your breathing from out your ass then? Matter of fact let me use your phone."

"Why something wrong with yours?"

"No, I let Devon use it, you know first girl and all."

"Go ahead but let me ask you a question first, I'm not trying to be funny or nothing like that, but did I just see your mother outside with something like a wig on? Everyone hears him and starts laughing.

"Ha, ha, hell just let me use your phone please."

"Use it for what? Is there something wrong with–I interrupted him, didn't you just ask me that? Let me speak it in Glucose, let me use your phone to call my girl."

"Oh, you know a word or two I see. Do you know the word no?"

While walking in the door Damion started mumbling. "I know a few more words. I appreciate that you are an unglazed ham looking mother…what you say D?"

"Huh, I didn't say anything."

"Yeah okay whatever."

He calls Kayla, "Hey what's up shorty?"

"Nothing just watching television."

"What are you doing?"

"Nothing just finish watching these fools messing around outside. I think we are going to Spingarn to watch a basketball game later. I would as if you want to come but I know you are on lock down. Just wanted to say don't drop the soap."

"Ha, I forgot to laugh, keep on making jokes about me being stuck in the house for some shit you got me in trouble for. We will see how that works out for you."

"You know how to say no."

"Really." Kayla begins to laugh condescendingly. "Oh, trust me I know now, you don't ever have to worry about that. "

"You say that now, but you're be calling me in the morning."

"Oh, you think you got it like that now. She starts to chuckle; a nigga gets a little taste and now he thinks he is running shit. Umm…can we use another word please? She begins to laugh even harder.

"So, you're telling me I don't have it like that? Wait a minute what's that you're listening too?"

"Our song boy, don't play."

"That does not sound like NWA: 100,000 Miles of Running."

"Really, that shit is not funny. Damn, why are you always on joke time."

"Because I am funny as shit."

"Bye boy."

"Okay, okay you know I'm just playing with you. I'm just trying to put a smile on your face. The real question is why you are always so serious?"

"Don't even try it, what you're not going to do is switch this on me."

"I'm just saying you are too young to be so serious definitely too cute. And I know our song by Baby Face."

"Why do you joke so much?"

"I don't know I guess it's a defense mechanism, or something who knows life can be so fuck up at times. At least that's what this shrink told me one time. Sometimes you have to make fun of it, because it can devour you."

"Did you just say you saw a psychologist?" Not realizing what he just said, He yells out shit in his mind.

"Hello, hello D you still there?" He starts to grin.

"Nah it wasn't like that it was a school trip. I vaguely remember but it was one of those science-educated ones."

"She interrupts him with laughter you were on a school trip. Yeah right! What an oxymoron."

"Ha, ha anyway before I died from laughter. All I'm trying to say is it's mean out here, bullets raining every night. It's enough to drive anyone insane, before you know it, you're the one with gun and pointing it to your head ready to pull the trigger. I do not want to ever think about the bullet that might have my name on it."

"Did your mother drop you on your head when you were a baby? Because there is something definitely wrong with you boy."

"I know I don't think it's that though. I believe it's the lack of sex."

"Bye boy." Damion starts to laugh. "Wait, wait! It was too late she hung up on him. "Well damn, that's twice she hung up on me. Let me call her back, I see you like hanging up on me?"

"Sure do, because I know it pisses you off."

"Are you going to call me later?"

"Maybe, maybe not, psych you know I am, D."

"I love it when you say my name."

After she hangs up the phone. He starts to sing. "Maybe a girl for you and a boy for me that is how much shit now I can't get this damn Baby Face song out of my head.

By this time Fats comes back into the living room.

"Man can you stop making love on my phone."

I'm off anyway I can't wait for you get some real ass and not that free government cheese line as pussy you be getting from Betty. So, you can release some of that tension in your fat." Damion puts his hand on Fat shoulder.

"I say this with love." He pushes his hand away.

"I see you been talking a lot of shit today since you got a little.

"Whatever, don't do that?"

"Do what?"

"Don't try to carry me because I'm always talking shit." "So, what's the deal for the night?

"We're going to the basketball game at Spingarn."

"Oh okay, that's what's up you know I'm down."

"Beside we have some business to take care of while we're down there."

"Business what kind of business?"

"Man, stay out of grown folk's business."

"Only business you should be concerned with is the business of getting some ass and stop living vicariously through me."

"Spell vicariously, smart ass?"

"Oh, shit that easy. Vicariously; y.o.u. n.e.e.d s.o.m.e a.s.s, vicariously see I can spell." Lowell comes out of the bathroom and interrupts their conversation. "If you two are finish we can leave now. Lowell walks towards the door, are you coming? Yeah in a little bit. Caught a little off guard, Damion keeps looking back towards the bathroom confuse.

"What...where did you pop up from?"

"I'm always in the shadows."

"Oh okay, Negro ninja you just getting off from work?"

"No, just getting in from happy hour if you must know."

"Who panties did you talk off tonight?"

"None, I have a woman or at least I think I have one."

"I know shorty is staying put. She likes you too much. I personally don't see it, whatever floats your boat I guess."

He grins and sits on the couch. Fats walks in asking Damion lets switch coats for tonight. He replies, with huh.

"If you can huh me you can hear me.

"Switch coats for what? You don't even like white. Besides, I just got it."

"I like the white coat though." Oh, the only reason I bought because it was the only color they had left. I don't know I haven't even gotten the feel of it yet."

"And I just bought mine last week, so what are you trying to say."

"Then why it looks like you were teething on it then."

"Are you going to switch or not?"

"What color is this anyway?"

"It's pale, pale green."

"What in the hell is pale green?"

"It is exactly what I said it is pale green."

"Come on, they exchanged the coats. Damn peer pressure is a mother. Why do I feel like I just got punk for my coat?" Lowell chimes in, what made you buy a white coat in the winter anyway? "Damion just stared at him. Anyway, all I know is you better be treating me to Wings & Wings later because I'm going be hungry as hell. They were walking through the door And Damion kept insisting on how much food he is going to need have to be fully satisfied." I'm getting double the mambo extra wings on the side, I'm about to eat like a king tonight. Fats ask him are you done yet.

"Nope I'm just getting started I want some fried rice, better yet chicken fried rice, oh yeah!"

"You sound like a fat person, keep eating shit like that, and you will be bigger than me."

"Shit, not in this lifetime you fat Brown Hornet." Damion begins to mimic the cartoon character voices.

The Night

As the sun mysteriously disappearing into the night, Damion notice a rare glimpse at the beauty of the moon. It was so big and so bright that night. Even though the temperature has fallen a little, the calmness of the dark made it a beautiful sight. As Damion look upward toward the sky, he felt that the stars were looking down on them. For some reason he felt a sense of invincibility that night like nothing on this earth could harm him.

They were on their way to Spingarn HS. They took a shortcut through Langston Terrace to meet up with rest of the fellas. They had some business they needed to take care of. Everyone was being so secretive and shit, Damion thought. The waiting had him reflecting on somethings and plotting on other things. It seemed like he was doing a lot of that today Boredom was not a passion of his. In addition, he had a lot on his plate, and he knew it was time for him to start taking things more serious especially with school. This was his senior year, and not trying to think about it made him think about it. Not realizing the fear was eating away at him. He did what he did best, wait until it smack him in his face at the last minute and handle it from there. He wonder what Kayla was doing right now probably thinking I'm up to something no good, especially when she is on lock down. I should call her; it is my fault anyway that she is on punishment. Then again, I think not I will just let her cool off for a day or two. It will probably drive her insane, better her than me. One day I will learn not to mess with other people heads like that. Not today though maybe tomorrow. He starts to look around, he had this overwhelming feeling that it's going to be a night to remember.

It was seven of them; Deon, Fats, Lowell, David, Tyrone, Troy and Damion. Damion mind begins to get fluttered with images of Kayla again. He starts to hum then sing faintly to himself. "A boy for me maybe a girl for you, that is how much. "Cuz, what in the hell are you doing?" Deon asks him.

"Oh nothing" Lowell starts to laugh, this nigga back here trying to sing. He thinks he is in love. Fats interrupts them, yeah with which one though. Everyone decides to laugh at Damion's expense. Thinking to himself, *got damn BabyFace I cannot get this damn song out of my head.*

"Hey, why are we walking anyway?" Damion ask.

"Why, you want to ride in my van?" David Answer.

"Not in this lifetime, no one trying to ride in the moist mobile."

"What's so funny Troy?" David ask.

"Your bama ass, especially with that ugly as Redskins starter coat on."

"Fuck you and those cowgirls."

"It is cool; you dead-skins can talk that shit now. We will be back on top again wait and see."

"Yeah right, more like that one and fifteen seasons again."

Lowell interrupts. "Yeah but that one win was against your skin's sorry asses." Then all hell broke out everyone started going back-and-forth with it.

"First of all, who is your quarterback and running back?" Troy ask Lowell.

"Troy Aikman is our quarterback; he was the number one pick in the draft."

"He won't be shit either."

"We will see this fall." As soon as they step on the school grounds, they finally stop yelling at one another. It was peaceful for a change, nothing but tranquility was floating in the air. Damion started humming again. Shortly afterwards everyone started singing the words to the BabyFace song. Maybe a Boy for you and a girl for me that is how much. They finally arrived at the school. There was a lot of people standing in line and some of them where wearing Cowboys and Redskins starter coats on. Which started the argument all over again. Now the whole line is looking at the boys from the hill as if they were crazy. Especially since football season has been over for about a month. This is how everyone reacts in this small part of the world when it comes to those two teams. It's God, money, and your football team. Damion begins to stare at the front door.

"What in the hell is this? They have security checking shit. Um...isn't this a high school game?"

"You know it's rough out here playa." Tyrone replies. "

"What they think the Hoyas are playing up in here? He abruptly stop talking when he thought he notice an odd face in the line. "What the hell." He hears a voice from behind him that startles him, but it's a familiar one.

"Hello D, how you're doing?

"Hey Crystal, I'm doing okay, just out here with the fellas."

"These are my cousins Dominik and Kendra."

"Hello Dominik and Kendra, how are you doing tonight?"

"We are doing okay." They both answered at the same time.

"What are you doing around here?" Damion ask her.

"I was going to ask you the same thing."

"I live around here. You live by Eastern don't you?"

"I do, I'm staying over my cousin house, off of Benning Road."

Now Crystal was, cute in the face, small in the waist, average body. She was an honor roll student probably one of the smartest kids in the school. However, she was a freak out of this world. Also, she was Damion first girlfriend in high school and in many ways, she was his first to his mind. At this point in Damion life led him to a crossroad. When she introduce her best friend to him, she became the second girl he ever had sex with and the second of many things. In addition to that when they introduce him to their other friend, she became the third girl he ever had sex with. After having flashbacks of all three. He thought to himself, *man I was terrible.* And in some way these women were the ones who pave this road of destruction for him towards women. He became more arrogant and cynical. You couldn't tell him anything after that. It was like his balls stock went up in the stock market. He thought, *it was funny running into her today of all days. Being though she was the first girl to ask him to go down on her. And to entice him even more she hit him with the jaw dropper. The Holy Grail of words, every man wants to hear, in any language. I'll suck your dick.*

It sounds good in French; Je te suce la bite. In Spanish; Quiero shupar tu pene. Latin; Ego ibo lac filio tuo dick. Even in Latin; Ergo ibo lac filo tuo dick. That shit was sounding good to me but for only a minute. Nah shorty I'm not in the eating pussy game, damn that. And on that note, I told her I'm out I'll holla. I guess times have changed. I always wonder if she ever found out about her friends and me.

"I haven't seen you in school lately."

"I've been mad busy with school projects trying to get ready for this next stage after school you know what I mean."

"I hear you, I just thought you were skipping class like you use to do when we were seeing each other."

"Pssh—what girl I have grown since those days it was hard at first but somehow, I got it done. And can I be honest with you, my lack the maturity was hindering me in so many ways. I was very immature, and I wasn't trying to do anything about it either. I'm still learning but I'm a different man now."

"Hmm I see. She circles him. Yeah you look real different right about now. I see you added some weight and gotten taller too." As she looks him up and down and squeezes his arm.

"Well what can I say I'm trying not to let my fans down out here?"

"Well you have my eyes wide open." Crystal and her cousins start laughing.

"What are you doing after the game?"

"Who knows probably get something to eat then chill." Finally, the line starts to move. "Well it's about damn time, they know this isn't our type of weather."

"So maybe we will see you later."

"Maybe you will." Damion starts strutting towards the door like he's the man.

After getting in and finding a seat. Everyone seems to go their separate ways and are enjoying themselves. The level of noise softens after the dancers come out followed by the band. The game begins and it was boring as hell to Damion.

"Why in the hell I'm here? Who was the genius who thought of this?"

"I did fool, now shut up I'm trying to watch the game.

"Shut don't go up"

"What you're ten now." A thunderous roar shook the bleachers as everyone begins to stand. It was a dunk that got everyone in a frenzy. It was something quite terrible, a three hundred and sixty degree spin dunk. Shortly afterwards it became a highlight real inside the gym. The crowed was going crazy, then came arguably the dunk of the game when a short guard dunk on a taller center. The game became more of a streetball game. The spotlight was on the game and Damion for as shy as he was, there were other times when he crave and yearned for it. It was like he had a split personality.

He see some kids from school. He give them some dap when one of these dudes proceeds to tell his boys some old back in the day story about him. When he use to fuck up words. And how everyone use to make fun of him. They all begin to laugh having a good time at Damion's expense. He feels dejected but he was playing it cool even though his temperature is rising with each word.

Once again, a fuse was lit in his eyes. It's on now so he started firing back. They were both roasting each other. Damion looks up and see another dunk. At this point he could care less about the game. He didn't really want to be there anyway. And he was just started to play his game.

Damion scans the kid body and sees multiple infractions. "No, this nigga didn't know you didn't." Everyone start asking what? No, this fool don't have the new Nikes on already. Why you trying to hide them. He moves the kid pants leg to the side and peels something off his shoe. Oh, no my bad those not Nikes he had on the upside-down Nikes. "Man, those are Nokes."

Everyone is laughing hysterically. Damion just went in on him even harder from there on it was a massacre. He was killing them in their section. He was on one of those rare roles, when everything you spit is on fire, like a Jedi knight. You know how niggas get though especially after getting there assess handed to them. Next thing you know their getting caught up in their panties and shit ready to fight. That's when you know their ass is done. Done like cook crack! Damion knew he wasn't going to trip off any of that bullshit anyway. They already knew they didn't want any part of him, they weren't insane. They already knew who he was and who he was with.

The game finally ended, and no one was happier than him. They started walking out of the building. He watches Crystal and her cousins standing by the door. He comes over where they proceed to ask him.

"What's up with you and your boys?"

"I don't know, we really haven't discussed anything yet."

"What are you about to get into?"

"Whatever you are getting into." Damion thought to himself, *shit she trying to get me into trouble.*

They started walking down the pathway, when he notice some of the fellas walking pass him. Crystal ask Damion aren't those your friends. That's when Fats walk by.

"You are always in some girl face."

"Why, you want to talk to them?"

"Why, they trying to do something?"

"That depends on you."

He tells Crystal to hold up while he holla at his boy for a sec. He started walking with Fats. "You trying to holla at one of them just let me know." That is when he felt that ominous feeling came over him again. He looks around when he observes a spooky figure in the background by the woods digging under a tree grabbing something and sticking it in their coat. All I know is that they had on an Eddie coat on. He was trying to make out his face when he hears his name from the distance being called. He turns and see its Crystal. When he turns back, the person vanished into the thin air. "Where in the hell did, they disappear too? And where did Fats go? Hold up Am I tripping?" Damion knew something was wrong or he was hallucinating, because it seems no one else saw any of this. He started thinking to myself *I'm probably just being a little paranoid or making something out of nothing.* He shakes it off and starts to hum again maybe a boy for me, shit I'm still humming that damn song. He started walking back towards Crystal, to tell her that they were trying to do something tonight. More like meet up later. Damion sees Moe and his man Rob. They all went to elementary and junior high school together. They were walking with their crew. Damion see Fats, and Deon stop them to talk. He tells Crystal to give me a second again, so he can holla at his man Moe. Nigga I haven't seen you since junior high.

"What's popping Moe?" While giving him some dap.

"What up my nigga, you know how we do."

"Right, right."

Impatience was written all over Damion face, when he ask Moe. "What is these niggas talking about now, I'm ready to go. Within a split second Damion life will be forever change. Fats swung on Rob, straight to his dome. Man, down and he was down. Life became primal, a melee ensued afterwards. Those who weren't running were rushing at each other. It was so many people out there it was hard trying to push people out of their way. A shadow grabs him from behind, however he was too strong for them he got out of it. Confusion was feeding on everyone like a hopeless victim. Damion didn't know if they were trying to stop him or trying to fight him. He just kept his head on a swivel. It all happen so fast there was no time to react. He went into survival mode animal instinct. He was trying to get back to the fellas when Moe and he ended up facing each other. Their hands where drawn as they begin to circle each other, a loud scream caught their attention. Both got a glimpse of what was happening to Rob. His man was being pummeled; He ran over to help him out. Trying to pull people out of there and off his boy. Rob was in the center of the circle. Where everyone was trying to stomp that dude into the ground.

They were trying to put him in the ground, just like they all stop. Damion looked upon them as if he already knew Rob was dead. He thought to himself, *no one could survive that stomping.* It was a Timberland boot stomp festival. After the festival was over everyone just walk away like nothing ever happen. There you have it in a nutshell the hood. Still in a confuse state of mind Damion wonders why in the fuck no one told him anything. They headed back to 21 street. While they were walking some old white dude wearing a physician coat gets in an Old dark tinted Chevy. He begins slowly next to them while playing Tears for Fears Mad World. Deon looks at Damion with a strange look on his face. Deon starts to reach for his weapon when the car makes a turn.

"What's up, you alright?"

"I don't know but for some reason I keep hearing that song."

"Now that you mention it, I've been hearing it too."

Lowell interrupts them. "You know what I heard it too, yeah back in eighty-four on what is call a radio. I'm sure you have heard of it."

Deon and Damion both look back at Lowell.

"What about you Fats?" Deon ask.

"Nope!" he starts laughing. "You keep listening to D crazy butt."

"Yeah, you do make a great point."

"So, that's how it's going to be. Eat a dick up to you hiccup." They all begin to laugh.

We met up with another group fellas from around the way. Suddenly everyone was outside cheering and patting these fools on their back. Like we just came back from a Viking pillage and Fats was Thor. They were all outside celebrating telling their part of the story repeatedly and drinking like crazy. While I'm still wondering what the fuck just happened. Fats Started walking towards me, to talk to me.

"I know you don't like to drink but why are you over here by yourself?"

"I don't know I'm just chilling and observing. You know I don't drink that hog piss anyway. I mean you go ahead enjoy your night I'm fine."

"You okay man seriously. Yeah, I'm fine just because I'm not joking around, doesn't mean there is something is wrong."

"I understand just checking on you. I thought to myself *there was something odd about today's events that transpired and all.* But I'm straight. Tomorrow will bring a new day."

Fats starts to drink straight from the bottle whatever you say and turns and rejoin his partners in crime. So, by now I'm getting told all the details of what went down. So, Big Mike who runs that block and area told Fats and Deon to pay Rob a visit. See Rob owe Big Mike around twenty grand. Now mine you Big Mike didn't want Rob dead. You know the old saying dead men can't pay no bills, so he instructed them too basically to break every bone in his body. I just shook my head its crazy out here. I guess in this game only the name changes, but the game remain the same, the game always remain the same.

Purgatory

amion continues to look at his surroundings, he couldn't help but to notice that the party light wasn't shining on everyone. For the fourth time today, he would receive that damn feeling again. He begins to panic. Trying to catch his breath he thought, *what's going on with me.* He looks around hoping that no one saw him. He looks to the right of him and see the fellas drinking and enjoying themselves. As he start to turn his head, he caught a glimpse of something in the corner of his eye. It appear to be some kind shadowy figures on the scaling the wall. He rubs his eyes, what the hell. He look again and it was gone and what was left where the faces that will haunt him for the rest of his life. They were the blank faces. The dark empty faces of the night, no joy no laughter no nothing, just emptiness. It is hard to see what truly lies in the hearts of most men. All Damion knew was, on that day there was nothing, but envy, malice and pure hatred worn upon their faces like masks. That death awaited any man that will ever dare to cross them. Then he notice the coats again from earlier two of them had the same ones on. He thought to himself, *this cannot be a coincidence, I do not believe in coincidences. I'm starting to get the feeling that I'm playing someone else's game and by their rules. Feeling like you're just a pawn in all of this.* Then again, he thought he saw a couple of people walking by with the same coat on. Maybe I'm over analyzing everything, just maybe. By this time, some of the fellas were starting to leave.

"Are you hungry?" Fats asks everyone.

"Yes, I am, and you know this I prefer Wings & Wings sir. In addition, let's not forget that you are paying for it. I have been waiting all night for this, thank you."

"Do not remind me, out here acting like a fiend over some food. Lowell interrupts their conversation. "Yes, I prefer some of that action as well."

The three of them headed to Wings & Wings. On the way he started to tell them his little secret. What he have been seeing and the shit that has been going on today. How he has been having these funny feelings all day like something bad is going to happen. "I mean some bad shit did happened today. Honestly, I do not know what in the hell is happening; you know what let me stop talking. Because right now I need to be focus on these wings B. I'm hungry then a mug."

Fats starts to laugh and tells him, "Sound like you cramping, and bleeding or is your mother condition rubbing off on you?"

Normally Damion would go the fuck off with any mentioning of Big C and him in the same breath. He was close though I mean he was fucking close! However, not this time, first he was exhausted, second, he was hungry, third it was the same as second he was hungry. With that said he still didn't allude to them everything. How today events where like a two-sided corn. On one side it was the best day of his life. On the other side he felt his life unraveling right before his very own eyes. He started thinking, *I do not know what's going on. Am I imagining all this shit I am too young to go crazy? Alternatively, maybe he is right maybe it is rubbing off on me.*

Before he knew it, they were walking in the door; they see Bobby and Kenny with a girl. Damion whispers fuck under his breath. Something is definitely wrong with these three. Fats looks at Damion. Bobby grew up with them, he used to live in Keisha building. In another life, they were all close friends. He moved to another neighborhood and stood with a different crowed, but we still ended up going to the same school. The notorious Brown Junior High school.

Somewhere out there in the universe someone thought it be genus to put all the worst kids the neighborhood together; the innocent, the set up girls, the crews and drug dealers in the same school. You had to be insane, or at least working on some type of social experiment. Putting them in an environment at a young age installing in them that they don't have any options other than killing one another. If you're taught that you're a cancer, eventually you will start believing it.

It was a breeding ground for future felons and sociopaths. And Bobby was well on his own way. Like they say money just show your true colors. The Eye of Horace has been corrupting souls since its conception. Then there was Kenny his right-hand man the thirteen year-old neighborhood stick up kid and hitman, who everyone hated and feared. The last time anyone of them heard his name is when he got stretched out on the ground with a 9mm jammed in his mouth. God must have been on his side that day because the weapon kept jamming. Instead he just got pistol whip severally.

Fats started talking, "What's going on Bobby?"

"Same old same you know nothing changes in this game, but the money from one hand to next. Introduced yourself baby," Bobby tells the girl standing next to him.

"Oh, hi I'm Zoe." She smiles.

They all said hey what is up. They were all talking while Damion ordered their food. Nevertheless, for some reason it was a little intense in there. Especially with Kenny staring at each of them as if, he had a problem. After receiving their food, Bobby and Kenny starting to get into it. Their voices where escalating with every word. While they were walking out of the door.

Lowell turns back. "Look at these fools, Fats and Damion look and observe Bobby girl yelling at him while Bobby was smashing Kenny head against the bulletproof glass. In addition, to add insult to injury while he was using his head as a meat grinder, he was still ordering his food.

"Aye mama-san I need six wings, fries, Zoe you still want something to eat baby."

"Damn strait. Let me get a half of steak and cheese and an order of fries? No wait um…let me see." Bobby holds Kenny head against the glass as he lets a scream out.

"No, I'll stay with my first order."

"You sure babe?"

"Yes babe." Fats tells them. "I hope he breaks that nigga face."

"Umm…well my wings are getting cold, so I am out. I have seen more than my share of head bashing today. And I don't want to see anymore." Damion starts walking, he yells back.

"Are you coming?"

"Man slow your butt down."

"What part of something is definitely wrong with those three you wasn't understanding?" They cross the 19th street and cut into an alley. Fats shakes his head.

"So now you're a fucking psychic ain't that a bitch."

"Whatever, the universe predicts you're going to be next." Damion makes this horror sound. He and Lowell starts laughing. "That shit isn't funny."

After exiting the ally Damion sees his cousin Peaches with Keisha. Keisha ask them where are you coming from; let me guess that nasty as Wings & Wings.

"And you know this man." Where is Deon?" Damion ask Peaches.

"I am not my brother's keeper. You know he's in these streets, that's where he always at. What's going on? You want him?"

"No just asking.

"What are you up to Peaches? "Fats ask.

"Nothing about to go in the house"

"Oh okay, I need to holla at you though."

"You know where I'm at."

"What you are doing out here?" Damion ask Keisha

"Don't let that bother you." He looks at her. 'I was just asking… you know what just forget it. I's always something with you."

"No, it is always something with you."

"How in the hell it's me." Peaches interrupts them. No, it's always something with both of you!"

"Nah that's her cuz. He starts to walk away.

"What was that mumbles." Damion stop dead in his tracks. Oh, shit Peaches whispers as she drops her head. Damion turns around with a dejected look of pain on his face. Lowell and Fats started tugging on him and telling him to come on.

"Why you keep letting her get under your skin?"

"Maybe because she is the anti-Christ. I'm done I can't do this anymore." Fats start laughing.

"No, you are not it is some weird kind of four play.

"What in the hell is so funny? What misery loves company? I got another question for you why is your ass so fat?" Fats laughter came to an extreme halt.

"What the fuck did you say?"

"You heard me fatback."

I'm going to let that shit slide today being though you got some pussy juice dripping from your lips. You're clearly not thinking at this moment. They just stood there face-to-face

"I am thinking clearer than I ever have you fucking waste of space. Lowell gets in between them. Fats spits and then smiles at Damion.

"Oh, it is not joke time now. Oh, that is a shame. If you weren't my boy." He shakes his head. "But check this out though do not let your mouth get you into something your ass cannot get out of." He bumps Damion when he passes him. As they continue through another alley, a strange sent overwhelmed them. They all look at each other. They knew the aroma of death was in the air, but something was different about it. Damion didn't know what it was, but it seem to be very old. It was so repugnant it felt that it was seeping through your pores and could taste it. It smelled vile vomit old rotten meat and blood and then some. Something was odd and it creepy was going on.

Finally, home, they are surprise because the front was full of people. Damion see Black, his brother and friends. Damion only thoughts were of selfishness. *What in the hell, they are out here like its eighty-degrees? All I know is I am not sharing my food with anyone.* "Do not even think about asking me got damn it." Can I and have, I want was all he heard. "No, no and hell to the no." He went straight inside to his mother's room. He begin to talk to himself. "Yes, peace and tranquility, turn this television on and watch some Miami Vice." For some reason, he was heavy in deep thought. *I wondered, do I really joke around that much or am I just masking a deeper problem. I mean I do know that there are times that;*

it seems I am missing something. Whatever that something is I don't know. Besides I'm young so who cares. The plan is to try and to get through the day the best way I know how. How do you get through life when it seems like it is a constant battle uphill and the obstacles in front of you get harder and harder? Oh well cannot dwell on life and its meanings, I'm starving. Therefore, he proceeded to go to work on those wings.

He was almost finish when he hears an often and so familiar sound outside. It was like thunder clashing against his walls. It was the sound of bullets echoing throughout his ears. It sounded like a war was going on. Damion jumps up to his feet while his food hits the floor. "That shit was awfully fucking close. Shit, I mean to damn close." He looks out the window and see people running across the street. It finally dawns on him. "Oh shit, everyone on the front my brother, my friends Fats." It was as if Damion was moving in slow motion trying to get to the door. His heart was pounding faster with each step. He never knew dread like that until that moment. He becomes motionless once he reaches the door. He can hear Fats mother yelling what is going on down there. In a faint voice, he hears Fats trying to yell, "I've been shot." Still standing in the doorway paralyzed, he tries to move but the hallway door seems to be moving further and further away from him. The door slowly opens its Fats falling to his knees their eyes connect. The horror look on his face as he proceeded to climb the steps. Had Damion in an unfamiliar world where his tears where hitting the air repeatedly. Mr. Richardson his next-door neighbor open his door and looks at Damion. He runs to the steps to help Fats the rest of the way.

Damion body gains consciousness again, he slowly walks up the steps. He slowly opens the door and look out to see if anyone else was hurt. To his astonishment, there was no one else hurt. Infect there wasn't anyone out there. He thought to himself, *thank God*. However, where in the hell did everyone go? The sirens begin to get louder as they approach. Damion see his cousin Deon running up to front looking distracted. The words no were being repeatedly when the police started to pop up out of everywhere out of nowhere. Coming through the alley up and down the street. They begin to yell towards Damion direction. Hey, you, do not move. Damion responded in a whisper; you're not talking to me. Therefore, he did what he always do the opposite of what anyone tells him too. He remove himself from the door and back inside his room. An hour passes when he emerges back outside. He see his brother running towards him with tears in his eyes.

"I heard the shots I thought it was you."

"No, it was Fats."

"Is he okay?"

"I don't know." His cousin comes back downstairs looking distraught.

"What happen?"

"He's been shot eight, nine, times I don't fucking know. He lost a lot of blood too. They are about to rush him to DC General."

"DC General!" Deon gives Damion an all familiar look. It was grim reaper time. Whomever was involved in this directly or indirectly will all pay with their lives. Damion thoughts were center back on Fats. *He's going to the stab and grab and die hospital. DC General where everybody dies, oh hell no. Where they have more bodies then the morgue.* William came back down hands dripping with blood I don't know about your friend they had to rip the coat off him. Rip the coat off him, what. They say it he looks too been shot ten or more times. Damion thought, it can't be not my man, and we just got into it, damn. He just stood there in disbelief.

Damion begins to converse with himself. He better survive because he's going to owe me another coat. I know I am wrong for thinking about the coat. No, you're not, the coat is taking your mind off him, your best friend. What am I going to do, without my friend my dog? His mind would not let him except any of this. He glances at his sister; tears are streaming down her face. Standing there like a statue he couldn't even console her. Eventually he walk into his room. David calls him and tells him.

"After walking Peaches back home from the store. Two guys with Eddie coats on where running in the opposite direction of the gunshots. It must have been an ambush."

"I don't think he even had his gun on him. They shot him up so many times you know they were trying to put him in the dirt." Damion begins to replay all the events in his head.

He found himself lying on the bed in complete silence staring at the walls. The gunshots repeatedly kept ringing in Damion's ear as he tried to get some sleep. However, sleep was his foe tonight. He got up and went to the bathroom to wash his face. Damion stares at himself in the mirror. He begins to feel uneasy when his reflection grins. What the F—His reflection reaches out of the mirror and chokes him before he could finish his words. The phone rings and Damion wakes up. The phone rings again. He glances at the radio clock and notice it's a couple minutes before midnight.

"Hello." He answered.

"Hey." It was Keisha.

"Hey what's up?" Damion notice she was crying.

"What's wrong? While trying to hold her tears back. Damion repeats his question.

"Are you okay D. I need to tell you something."

"What is going on?"

"Your cousin Deon was in a shoot-out; he has been shot multiple times. They rush him to the hospital; they said he passed out from losing a lot of blood from fighting and trying to get away. They found him slump over in his car crash into someone house in Trinidad."

"H—he what…wait a minute, what, stop playing. That shit is not funny." He could hear her sobbing in the background I am not joking. Reality sets in.

"Where is Peaches?"

"She is on her way to the hospital."

"What hospital and do not say that fucking DC General."

"Yeah, I think so I am not sure though.

"No! This can't be fucking happening. The phone mercifully hits the floor. He could not grasp none of this at the time. A soft and familiar voice is still coming through the phone. "Hello D, hello D, are you there?" He started panting as room began to spin, the only visions he saw was of a dark an obscure one. Is this death! He begins to whisper to himself.

"Damn it, am I next." He didn't envision none of this happening. Nothing bad ever happens to my friends or family He just sat there in shock. Is this, the beginning, or is it the end, he wondered. His started having flashes but they were backwards. His world was going in reverse starting with the shootings.

The arguments with Fats to Keisha the fights taking pictures, Black, Kayla to himself until there was nothing but complete emptiness. His life just started to fade into darkness. Dear God, please help me.

An hour later, he still could not fall asleep; he was still in so much pain and anger. He never felt so hopeless in his life. Analyzing the images flowing throughout his mind. He thought, *what did I miss, there where so many signs? Why I didn't act sooner? Why didn't I try harder to convince them that something was going to happen?* Pacing back and forth continuing thinking to himself. *Maybe I was scared. Fearing that I was going crazy like my mother, more then I really would admit. I don't know damn it!* So many emotions where erupting inside of him. Feeling hungry he started walking towards the kitchen. He stops dead in his track because he already knew, there wasn't any food in the refrigerator. He opens the refrigerator to find nothing but space, bread, Kool-Aid and water.

"Fuck!" He shakes his head.

"I'm not trying to walk especially after the shit that is going on tonight. And nobody delivers to this neighborhood. I need to get some air." He begins to look for his clothes. After getting dress Damion opens the door and look at the outside front door. He hears the wind blowing against the door making it sound creepy.

"Hello, is anyone out there. Am I'm tripping?" A cold chill spiral down his spine.

"What the hell, oh I forgot my keys." He closes the door and starts to look for them.

"Is anything where I put them at anymore damn, I finally find them." He headed back to the door.

"Why is the door open…didn't I just close it? I know I'm tripping now." He walks outside and started to look around.

"Man, its cold out here. He hesitates for a second then walk to the front of the fence. He just stands there fixating on the crime scene tape.

Wake Up

After stumbling out of the bathroom. Damion hears his sisters arguing.

"I thought it was Saturday" He mumbles. His brother walks by.

"No, it's a weekday, time for school."

"Today is Saturday so I'm going back to sleep." Damion begins to pull the covers over his face.

"Today is Thursday." You forgot two days."

"Wait a minute, is mom home?"

"No, she called and said she is working a double shift." Damion pulls the covers from over his head.

"Boy what is you talking about?"

"I'm talking about today, its Thursday."

"Thursday, what…wait it can't be I thought yesterday was Friday."

He sat back up with this puzzle look on his face. He kept thinking, *why don't I remember.*

"Well we are off."

"Good that's all I want to hear." A dark ominous voice whispers out.

"There is no memory here in this place." With confidence in his voice Damion asks.

"Where is this place you speak of?"

"Well hell silly."

Damion hears the door close, which wakes him up. Then the door reopens and close again. He yells.

"Stop opening and slamming the door!" He can hear his sisters laughing as they exits the apartment, slamming the door once again.

"Damn girls, this must be—I'm not about to finish that sentence." He finally gets up, well sit up, and turns on the television. He begins to watch videos on The Box. He was thinking, *damn, they are killing this Digital Underground joint to death." Rhythm Nation by Janet Jackson hmm let me check this one out.* The video plays for a minute.

"Damn Janet is that you. You gotten sexy as hell." He started singing the song to Rhythm Nation. Feeling hungry he gets up to go to the kitchen. As soon as he opens the door shit, I knew it. He stood there with the door open. He thought, *I could have sworn I already did this. Déjà vu I guess oh well Captain Crunch it will be. What, damn it, who leaves an empty box. You Negroes are worthless.* He jumps into the shower and gets dress. Still humming Rhythm Nation, he walks out the door and up to Fats apartment. Oh, shit I forgot he's not home. He walks back outside and down the steps when he hears someone yelling his name repeatedly. He looks around.

"D, are you deaf?

"Oh, what up dog?"

"Nothing man I am just chillin." It was his boy Antonio from around the way. They have been going to the same school since Charles Young Elementary.

"What have you been up too, besides not going to school?"

"Well you know how I do."

"Yeah, I know, I been trying to holla at you. Man, I wanted to thank you for the hooking me up with o' girl too."

"What girl, who are you referring too?"

"Your mama, you forgot already?" He started laughing.

"Ha, ha hell," He said with a puzzle frowned.

"Seriously, you don't remember the shorty Adriana at school?"

"Oh yeah, the girl with the big backyard and the miniskirts. Man, you're straight it was a favor for my girl that's her peeps."

"Backyard fat as hell. While making big c-motion with his hand. Man let me tell you what happen though. You know Mr. Williams is still out on leave, and we had a new substitute teacher. Okay school let out and I am at my locker when she comes behind me and cover my eyes.

"Hey baby, what going on with you today?"

"You know it's you girl."

"You sure it is me."

"I wouldn't have said it if it wasn't true."

"Oh yeah, prove it then." She had this look in her eye.

"Oh yeah, so I grab her hand and took her to the back of the classroom."

"No one was there?"

"Nope that was the best part." The substitute already left for the day. So, I kindly lock the door behind us. That is when she jumps me. We were sitting in Mr. Williams chair kissing.

"Stop playing, you for real?"

"I'm not making this up. She asks me if, I wanted to see something. Hell yeah, you know I do." She turns around and lifts her skirt.

"Are you for real?"

"Hell, to the yeah."

"Whatever nigga you are lying like shit."

D, I am trying to tell you this shit is for real. Hold up I haven't told you the best part yet. Therefore, after the visual display, she gets on top of me and we started kissing again. D we were going at it. Then she grabs my joint and pulls it out. I am like, oh shit it is on now. You know I'm trying to hit now."

"Do not tell me you did it in the class."

"I wish! She were not having that though."

"So, what happen then?" She tells me she knows a place. I am thinking well let us roll then. We go upstairs on the old abandon side of the school. We go inside this hidden room by one the classroom. It was a little dusty in there. I started grinning. So, this is it.

"Are you serious you really did it?

"You know it. I put my coat down and then I put it down." That was until those big as rats chase us out of there. Both of us running with half our clothes on. Damion looks at Antonio with a weird look on his face. Rats. They both burst out in laughter.

"I know it sounds crazy but it's the truth."

"Man, shorty is a straight up freak.

"I know but she is mine though."

"I hear that, so where are you going now?

"Where you think? At the same time, they both say Adriana house. They started laughing again.

"Antonio you lucky as shit. My girl only knows, no, don't, stop and quit it." As he shakes his head.

"Well what can I say when you got it you got it."

"Whatever, you don't have to rub it in. I'll holla at you later. I am going to get something to eat."

"All right holla at you later. Damion continues back on his quest for food. He continue to walk down I street.

Devan and Aliyah

eading towards the mall, he notice a car with tenant windows. Who in the hell is this; already paranoid he kept on walking. He hears the car coming to a screeching halt.

"Aye D what up boy?" Damion look back.

"What the…boy I didn't know who in the hell that was. Seems like I am running into everybody today."

"Yeah check out my new shit." He walks around the car.

"Mint green Max, nigga this joint is clean as hell."

"Where you off too?"

"Trying to get something to eat."

"Hey, I know this new spot downtown I think it is called the Lincoln's Waffle Shop."

"Sounds good to me."

"Yeah, we been trying to get something to eat ourselves."

"Who is we?" Dread crawls all over his face.

"You Okay?"

Oh, you heard me; he looks down at the car. He whispers to himself repeatedly, please do not let it be Aliyah please do not let be Aliyah. The window comes down, it's Aliyah. *Damn it* portrayed his thoughts. There was a long emphasis on the two words.

Hey A—Aliyah.

"Why is you saying my name all like that? You knew who it was stop playing with me boy. You are irritating me already boy

"Boy, who are you calling boy?"

"You boy! Are you getting in or what?"

Damion lowers his head.

"Shit not these two. Reluctantly he tells them he is in." Aliyah started yapping her trap.

"Hey, it is too early for that BS Aliyah.

"What I am just minding my own business. Damion gets into the car thinking to himself *what, am I getting myself into today.* Devan ask me, where's Fats?

"He is in the hospital."

"For what?"

"Do I look like my brother's keeper? Aliyah pulls out a three-eighty mm gun.

"This is my brother's keeper right here. The problem solver baby."

"Awe that's cute." Aliyah starts to speak in Jamaican dialect (Patios). Damion looks at her with a confuse look on his face.

"What is that even supposed to mean? Devan just kept driven, while Aliyah started talking to her weapon.

"Damn you are sexy as hell baby.

"You like it don't you baby? Tell me how much you like it."

"What the hell." Damion just sat there looking at them both wanting to slap the spit from out of their mouths. See the problem with these two is that they are crazy as fuck and can be very volatile; anything can set them off especially Aliyah. You would think as fine as she is, she would be chilling somewhere on a date, partying or falling in love or something like that. Not this chic she like stabbing, robbing and shooting. Anything of that magnitude gets the chic turned on. She's been stab twice and shot three times. Damion has been knowing my Devan since McFarland junior high summer camp. A school located on Georgia Avenue North West DC. He was already doing crazy shit back then. Damion recalls a moment in time when he saw Devan eating dirt. He thought, how a person can reason with a nigga that eats dirt. Well this is the story or tragedy, of Devan and Aliyah.

How he met Aliyah, there story started a little over a year ago. Devan was throwing his cousin Mike a birthday party over Mike house. And wouldn't you know it the parents were out of town that weekend. Aliyah and her two cousins came through, they were from Sursum Corda. There were a lot of activities going on to say the least drinking, smoking and fighting. He had to throw one of the dudes out of his cousin house after whooping his ass first. Some dudes can't take a joke. Devan was cracking jokes earlier on his shoes. Dude swung and got punish for it. He enters the room when they begin to play some reggae music. After playing go-go for about two hours straight. That is when Aliyah and her cousins took over the party. Devan glances over and notice Aliyah for the first time.

The crowd started moving back to give them some room and they went to work. No one at the time seen moves like that before maybe because their family where from Jamaica. They were dancing to Sister Nancy, What a Bum. Aliyah noticed Devan and when their eyes locked, it was like some Romeo meeting Juliet. They just sat there talking majority of the night. By now the party was winding down, there were about ten people still in there. Aliyah and Devan where on the floor slow dancing to Can You Stand the Rain by New Edition. When the door pops open and two masked men started letting loose. Round after round zip through the air. He turns Aliyah around to shield her from being hit. She still ended up being shot and so did he. He was shot twice in the back. However, they were the lucky ones. Five people were injured and three more were found dead including

Aliyah's cousin. The two shooters fled but not before Devan, blackout he'd remember those where the shoes of the nigga he threw out of his cousin house. He said he was going to comeback. He didn't think he was going to comeback like that. A month has pass and Devan and Aliyah had the lust for vengeance in their eyes. They begin to ruffle a few feathers on their revenge spree. It took a while, but it work. They finally found out where the dudes lived. A week later, they were park outside one the dude's house.

"What are we waiting for Devan?"

"Baby calm down I told you his mother is in there I am waiting for her to leave I do not want to hurt any innocent bystander. I know her schedule she is leaving around 10:00.

However, it is 10:30 now.

"Fuck that my cousin is six feet deep in the ground and she was an innocent bystander. Because of that bitch as nigga, he didn't give a fuck. You think I'm going to give a fuck about his mother that bitch is dead too." She pulls her gun out and up to the window and points it up in the air.

"When I see her, I am going to shove this joint so far up in that cunt's pussy, she is going to get fucking pregnant. I'm going to make her wish she was pregnant by my gun for having a bitch as nigga for a son. Devan looks at Aliyah.

"Baby I love it when you talk so fucking nasty, that shit turns me on." They started kissing uncontrollably and passionately.

"Damn baby you got my shit all wet."

"Oh yeah, we are going to have to do something about that later. Come on, as they begin to open the door."

"Holdup, who is that?" A woman walks pass the car. "

"That's his mother. It's time baby." They broke into the house with ease. While silently walking through the house they begin to hear music playing. It was Somebody Watching Me by Rockwell was playing. They heard more noises coming from upstairs, Devan points upstairs and whispers to Aliyah to split up secured the bottom then we will work our way upstairs. A male voice yells out from upstairs.

"Hello, mom are you still here?" After clearing the other rooms, they hear more sounds coming from upstairs. It was the sound of footsteps.

"Mom are you still here?" Aliyah hid in the living room as the footsteps got closer.

"Damn she left already." He started walking towards the kitchen talking to himself. He opens the fridge let us see what is up in here. He grabs carton of milk and starts drinking from it. The fridge closes and the last thing he saw the butt of a gun coming towards his head. He hits the ground and milk splashes everywhere on the floor. He wakes up confused, groggy and in pain. The pain was coming in the form of punches Aliyah was giving him. He looks down at the tape around his wrist and ankles.

What's going on? Why are you doing this?"

"I see you have amnesia huh. You don't remember my baby?"

"No!"

"Wrong fucking answer." She then takes the butt of the gun slaps the taste out of his mouth.

"Fuck you!" She proceeded to slap his face a few more times. Feeling groggy, he asks Devan.

"You woman wear the pants nigga?"

"I'm not a violent man by nature. Devan eyes widen.

"However, I love the purity of it. The raw emotion of it, it's more than I can bare sometimes." The victim starts to tremble in fear, as he looks at them.

"Man, I didn't do anything."

"I hear you, all we want is some info. And we heard you were the one to get it from.

"Whatever you need I will tell you."

Oh, we know baby we know. Aliyah tells him as she rubs his face. Tears swiftly flowed down his cheeks followed by screams. They found both dudes bodies in a different alley with the same mo. They were torture with their tongue cut out, ears chop off and their eyes burnt out. Speak no evil, hear no evil, and see no evil.

It is always something crazy with these two. They were getting out of the car.

"Oh, it is by the Lincoln theatre. I haven't been downtown in a while." Damion interjects.

"It's been going downhill for years. Devan replies.

"I know, it seems like all the stores are closing up shop and everyone is moving out. Before you know it, DC will not be nothing but a wasteland."

"It is pancakes time now." They sat at a table in the back of the dinner. Aliyah just kept rambling on an on baby this baby that. Just shut the fuck up please, was what Damion wanted to yell out, but he just suffered in silence instead. After eating Devan ask Damion if he was trying to go to the movies with them at Union Station.

"Yeah that's cool. What's playing?"

"That new Steven Seagal movie."

"Oh yeah, Hard to Kill right. Cool with me if Aliyah can hold her breath for one second, I'm down."

"What, hold these punks?"

"Whatever, bumbaclout girl. Let me call my girl so she can meet us up there."

"What?" Call me that name again and see what happen."

"Anyway, Damion responds in a condescending way. He walks over to a pay phone when he hears Devan and Aliyah arguing.

"You just going to let him talk to your baby like that?" He glances at Damion with a funny look on his face. Damion raises his shoulders up to gesture he didn't do anything with a smirk look on his face.

"Are you going to defend my honor by killing him?"

"You want me to kill him? Not stab him or take his eye out. Nor cut his tongue out."

"Ooh I like the sounds of that. Let's do that one baby."

"I don't know about that babe, he's one of my closest friends. You know I don't have a lot of them.

"I know baby. At least he won't be dead. He just won't be able to talk."

"You know if we do this, his cousin is going to come after us.

"If it's our time, then we to shall go out in a blaze of glory."

"Hmm I still don't know babe."

"You still don't know." What do you mean you don't know?"

Damion interrupts them.

"She said she would meet us up there. They all get in the car Damion sits in the backseat with a smile on his face enjoying the endless silence.

"What's wrong baby?" Devan asks Aliyah.

"Don't baby me now."

"What did I do now?"

"You know what you did. Whatever just drive."

"That's what I'm doing."

"Yeah like a girl."

"I hear you, but you know you love it though."

"Whatever you say."

They arrived at Union Station and park in the garage Devan and Aliyah where still going back in fourth with each other. They each got on the escalator one by one with Aliyah in front. There were three girls coming up the escalator. The first of the three girls started staring at Aliyah.

"Take a picture it will last longer bitch!" Aliyah yell.

"Who are you calling a bitch?" The first girl yelled back.

"Bitch you bitch. Pick one or all three it don't make a difference to me." Aliyah flashes that devilish smile of hers. Damion thought to himself, *oh hell here comes crazy time.* The three girls came back down the escalator and followed Damion and them until they caught up with them. Too much surprise they were all in shock. One of the girls even took a step closer to Aliyah waving her finger in the air.

"Bitch you don't won't any of this trust me on that shit." We from 18th and D we don't play that shit."

Devan grabs Aliyah by the arm as she takes a step towards the three girls.

"I am trying to go see Steven Seagal. We can play with these bitches another time."

"Bitch, I know this Ralph Tresvant looking as nigga ain't talking shit too. Devan turns around with a smile.

"Oh, that was kind of funny. He begins to pace back and forth.

"You know what else is funny or shall I say smell funny. Have any of you ever smell a body when it's riddle with bullet holes." Aliyah flashes her 380MM handgun. All three of them took a step back. A couple of people walking by saw what was going down but kept it moving.

"That gunpowder and lead eating your rotten corpse. Aliyah interrupts Devan.

"Baby, let me have all three of them please?" Devan looks back at Aliyah and then the three girls.

Okay maybe you can have two of them. The big one and the little one. By this time the girls were looking little scared and starting to tremble in fear.

"No, hmm–decision decisions. You can have one." Aliyah charges at the three girls as they all started to run. She grabs one of them by their hair.

"You are mine bitch." But the only thing she had in her hand was a wig. Damion and Devan started laughing so hard they both had tears in their eyes.

"That shit isn't funny!" She yells as she shakes the wig. They all started laughing after that.

"Damn baby I wanted them too."

"I know baby. He hugs and consoles her.

"There is always next time."

"You promise?"

"Yes baby, I also have something else for you too. You can have his tongue, only his tongue.

Yes baby, I love you so much. They begin to kiss patiently. Aliyah turns and looks at Damion and flashes that devilish smile again. Damion instantly stop laughing. As they walk down another flight of escalators Aliyah started smelling the wig

"Ooh this smell like ass. She tosses it to the side. We finally get downstairs. Damion tells them he's going in Sam Goody.

"Can we do it now?"

"Not now babe, I want to see the movie first."

"Okay baby." Damion receives a beep from his pager. Its Kayla he calls her from a payphone. To tell her to meet him in the food court. But there was no answer. He thought she probably is already on her way. In that short period of time he went looking for his mind because the two were driving him insane with the constant arguing and making up, all in the same breath. He catches up with them.

"Will you two chilled out, got damn. Get a room or something."

"I see someone isn't getting any. Aliyah replies.

"You don't have to worry about me you demon seed. That's when Kayla walk up.

"Hey baby." Damion stands up and hug her. Whispering, hey these two are insane. She's probably thinking of a way to kill me other that you will be okay. He turns around and introduce her to Bonnie and Clyde.

Damn D, I didn't know you were pulling them in like that. She is fine." Aliyah says. Kayla smile and sits down.

"Thank you and tells Aliyah she has a pretty name."

"I like her. So how did you end up with this fool?"

"D is the sweetest person I know. I mean do not get me wrong he has his issues."

"A lot of them I am sure. In the end, he has always been kind and good to me."

Umm I am still here, and I can hear you. You do know, that right?"

Yes, boy Kayla answers. She stands up and grab his hand.

"Come on boy."

The movie was pack. He thought to himself, *it is early, and this joint is full. It's going to be good.* There were no seats together, so we sat in different sections of the theater. They started watching the movie and it was getting good. When Damion started to hear some whispering from the couple behind them. He paid it no mind at first and kept watching the movie. As time passes, the dude was starting to get a little louder. Even though he was starting to hit that nerve. He just look at Kayla and turned back to the movie screen. See the problem was Damion was that guy. All loud at the movies cracking jokes making everyone laugh. He would put on a comedy show he love that crap. If no one else understood he did. That's why he was trying to remain patient. However, it was wearing thin. He notice Kayla is starting to get mad herself. After Damion look back and gave them that look. Everything seem to get a little quiet. Until he started telling the plot of the story. And what happening next. He lost it after that.

"Dude really, shut the fuck up; my girl and I are trying to watch the movie."

"Huh….what nigga?"

"Nigga if you can huh you can hear. You heard what the fuck I said rambling on and on like a fucking bitch and shit."

"Nigga fuck you; I say what the fuck I want to say and do what the fuck I want to do."

"Oh yeah." Damion starts to move when Kayla grabs his arm. By this time, everyone has stop watching the movie and started observing them.

That is when the usher comes over is everything okay gentleman. They both went off on him.

"If you do not get your bitch as out of my face."

"Everything is cool get the fuck out of here." Damion says. The usher leaves out. The both of them started going back and forth again. Damion becomes a little paranoid because this nigga is sitting behind him with an advantage. If he decides to do something, he got me. He thought to himself, *he wasn't about that life, shit he just putting on a show for his girl. Because if he was trying to do something, he would have done it by now.* It didn't really matter anyway because the usher came back with the police. White boys they will snitch on you in a heartbeat. The police stood there the rest of the movie. As the movie was, nearing its end Kayla put her hand into Damion's and whisper in my ear.

"Thank you." She kisses him on the cheek. He looks at her and she smiles. He thought, *if every day was like this it could be something special.* Then you remember that your girl is a jealous, paranoid schizophrenic. He smiles and wink at her. Who knows, nothing is written in stone he saw a beautiful side of her today a side he forgot. He thought *maybe if I keep my head right maybe this side of her will stay.*

After the movie was over, Devan and Aliyah comes over.

Hey, what was all the commotion about? Nothing some fool talking reckless. He was talking all through the movie. Oh, that bama shit you be doing. Funny, I forgot to laugh, it's cool though. As they started walking out Devan ask.

"So, where are they?" Damion looks at him for a second and continues to walk towards the exit.

"They already left. You don't have to worry about them." Before Damion could utter another word. Kayla blurts out.

"No there not I can see them right there. She begins to point at them. Aliyah grabs Devan hand.

"Come on baby let's go. Are you two coming?" Kayla and Damion answers were total opposite of each other. He said no, and she said yes. He looks at her confuse. Devan and Aliyah leaves but not before she says, I see a lover quarrel about to brew.

"Shorty are you crazy? Why would you show Bonnie and Clyde where they were? I told you they are crazy as fuck, and not crazy like you, I mean literally crazy. I am talking certifiable insane, now I must go and check on these two before they get us all lock up. I can handle my own mess I do not need any help from them. Trust me when I say they're not doing it for my benefit. They get high off that crazy as shit." Damion starts walking away from her; he looks back and see her trying to follow. He stands in front of her.

"Where do you think you are going?"

"With you, I'm going to help protect my man."

That's cute, I appreciate that. He smiles. Shorty, I do not need any protection."

"I'm still going."

"Baby you are sweet but if you do not sit your cult going as down."

"Being catholic is not a cult."

"Really, you say tomato I say cult, regardless you still aren't coming."

"See that's the problem right there everyone is always trying to shelter me and tell me what to do. My family, friends the church. Now you, I am getting tire of that shit."

"I am not trying to shelter you or anything like that. I'm just trying to keep you out of harm's way this is not a movie. This here is real some real shit, and when those bullets start flying, they don't never carry a name on them. If I knew how to get out of this hellhole, I would but I don't. It have to be something better out there than this crap." He shakes his head.

"So, you trying to get in. I'm just trying to understand that. Why you are so fascinated by it."

"What do you mean I am already in? I live around the corner from you, not another country, just around the corner. Just because my family situation is better, and my upbringing is different. Doesn't mean I don't live in the same hellhole. I witness the same atrocities, and genocidal events you see." He steps closer to her. "I would never belittle your experience baby. You are one of the few good things in my life that I need." This is what you call irony I guess, the jokester being serious for a change." She begins to smile.

"I know right." He kisses her on the forehead.

"Give me a minute, I'll be right back. He smacks her on her butt. It's jingling baby."

"Go head daddy." She replied.

"That's my girl." He headed off looking for Bonnie and Clyde. He begins to talk to himself. "Where did they go, I know they had to walk this way?" He headed back in the opposite direction. Damion hears some strange noises. "Where is that noise coming from? Sounds like it's coming from the bathroom." The noise begins to escalate louder as he approaches the door. Damion is startle by another loud noise sounding like a radio. He turns and walk towards the balcony and look over it. He see six cops walking underneath them. Shit was his first thought. He walks back to the restroom and observes Devan kicking the shit out of the dude from the movie theatre.

"I knew you were coming faking like you don't like this. Shh Damion puts his finger over his lips.

"The police is below us. Where is Aliyah?"

"In the women's bathroom." They started walking out the restroom but before they left, something dark came over Damion. He tried to kick the life out of dude. They both walk into the lady's restroom where they see Aliyah squatting over the girl with the 380 in her mouth. Damion goes to the door to look out.

"Baby the police are close. So, we need to leave." Devan tells Aliyah.

"I'm not going anywhere. The girl starts crying trying to talk. Aliyah pulls the gun out of her mouth.

"What did you say baby?"

"Please don't kill me please don't kill me."

"Come on baby it's time to go."

"Okay just one more thing she squeezes the trigger. The girl started crying louder.

"Shh baby today wasn't your day today lucky for you." Damion looks on with relief in his eyes. Aliyah gets up and they all walk out.

"I thought you said the police where coming Damion points down, they begin to look over the rail. One of them saw him.

"I think one of them said they needed to use the bathroom. Alright Devan it's time to go." Devan grab Aliyah by the hand it's time to go baby.

"Oh, shit Kayla, I will meet you at the car." He gets to the stairs and look back; he see the cops walking towards the bathroom. He started to pick up the pace going towards the food court. He see Kayla below him.

"Hey say hey sexy. Kayla looks up and smile.

"Hey you." Damion had this bad feeling and looks behind him. He see the cops talking on the radio pointing in his direction.

"Damn!" He yells.

"Meet us on the side off the metro entrance on the side street now. She look confused. However, she got the picture when she saw him running. He nearly ran into two cops, but they didn't see or hear him. He hid by the escalator where they couldn't see him. He can hear the radio reporting; be on the look for three teenagers. Two boys and a female. He needed to get upstairs. A couple started arguing and pushing each other, the cops walk over there to intervene, it was like a divine intervention. He walk right past them like nothing happened. Finally, he get to the car. Devan starts to pull off.

"Where is Kayla? Aliyah ask. I know you didn't leave her?"

"No, I told her to meet us on that side street where the other metro entrance is at."

They were coming down the ramp when they see more of Capitol Hill finest pulling up. They just drove right past them.

"This the street right here?"

"Yeah, why are you stopping?"

"Man, it's a one way and cars are coming up.

"Do what you do best be crazy."

"Just drive baby." Aliyah yells. They nearly hit two cars on the way down Devan hitting the horn like crazy. They see Kayla and she is running like an US Olympic track star. She is yelling they are behind me. Damion open the back door and while Devan slows down. Miraculously she jumps right into his arms safely. She closes the door behind her, and they were off. Damion can feel her heartbeat pounding in his hands. She tries to talk while trying to catch her breath. He leans in and tell her.

"I'll be your air. He kisses her. Doing the kiss, she starts to grin.

"What, to corny?" Everyone starts laughing.

"Devan, I want to breathe the air you're breathing baby."

"I can't do it unless we breathe it together." More laughter ensued. Damion had to laugh himself. Kayla whispers in Damion ear. "I never felt so alive." They drove to North Capitol and K Street when

"Aliyah, you feel like going home." Damion interrupts abruptly.

Hell no, man no one is trying to roll up into the stab and grab.

"What?" Aliyah turns angrily.

"Oh, my apologies, what I meant to say no one is trying to go to Sercum Cordas. Only because we need to go uptown." Aliyah looks back at Devan

"Before we were rudely interrupted, I was about to say no." She looks back at Damion.

"No, I don't feel like dealing with my folks right now."

"Well we can go over my house, are you cool with that D?

Yeah you can drop me and Kayla off at my grandmother's house and pick us up when you finish."

"Sounds like a plan." Devan looks at Aliyah after looking in the rear mirror at Damion and Aliyah. She smiles at Devan and gives him a look that said don't worry about it. He grins and keeps driving. Damion never knew he almost lost his tongue that day.

"Where do your grandmother live?"

"Right off Georgia Avenue. Where going uptown baby." Kayla moves closer to Damion as he puts his arm around her. On our way uptown, they started falling asleep as the radio started to play, Just to Keep You Satisfied by Marvin Gaye. Devan was telling Kayla and Damion they were at his grandmother house.

"Hey Kayla, wake up." They got out of the car.

"Hey, call the house when you are ready. Devan told them.

"You sure? Y

"You know your grandmother don't like me".

"Just call the house."

"Cool we will hit you up later."

"Nice house." Aliyah tells Damion

"Yeah, I stayed here from time to time that's how Devan and I met."

Grandmas House

Damion started knocking on the door but there was no answer. He knew they had to be in there. He noticed both of their cars outside. He begins to knock again. After a few more knocks his grandmother comes to the door.

"Hey baby."

"Hey grandma."

"Come on in. And who is this?"

"Oh, this is Kayla my girlfriend."

"Oh wow, she's very pretty."

"Thank you, Mrs. Jones you have a lovely home."

"Thank you, baby, you two are a long way home."

"Yeah, we were hanging out with Devan."

"Boy didn't I tell you to stop hanging around that demon seed. That boy is nothing, but trouble infect the whole family is."

"He isn't that bad grandma." Even though he knew better than that.

"Yeah keep telling yourself that. So, what's going with you two?" Before Damion could answer his grandfather comes into the living room.

"Boy we haven't seen you in a while, so what do you want?

"I don't want anything."

"Right answer because we don't have anything, no money or any food. So, who is your friend?"

"This is Kayla."

"Hello Mr. Jones, how are you doing today?"

"I'm fine, pretty and polite. May I ask you a question?"

"Yes sir, what is it?" What's a tenderoni such as yourself doing with my grandson you lose a bet or something." Aliyah looks at Damion and begins to blush. She starts to laugh trying to explain. While Damion says the word tenderoni under his breath in shock. His grandfather starts to laugh as well. Sweetheart I'm just messing with you. Damion grandmother shakes her head while his grandfather walks back into the room to finish watching television.

"Are you hungry? I just got finish cooking some catfish." He looks towards the room and whispers.

"Oh yeah, you know that's my favorite." Kayla tells her, no thank you Miss Jones.

"I'll be right back." He hears his grandfather coming back into the living room. Damion picks up a magazine and started reading it.

"Boy who you think you fooling with the magazine is upside down. When she ask you if you wanted something to eat? What were you supposed to say?"

"No."

"I can't hear you. What you say?" As he places his hand around his ear.

"I'm supposed to say no."

"So, why did you say yes then?"

"Because she's making catfish." He just stared at him.

"We make enough food for the both of us and that doesn't include your greedy ass. His grandmother comes back out with a plate and cup in her hand.

"Woman what are you doing?"

"Hush old man and leave these kids alone."

"Do not tell me to hush woman, I am the king of this castle. He walks back to the bedroom talking out loud.

"I work too hard, damn kids always wanting something. First, it was our kids now it's their kids."

"Do not pay him any mine. He just mad he isn't getting any."

"TMI grandma." Kayla starts to grin.

"Oh, hush boy. So, what brings you here?
She looks at Kayla are you pregnant?" Damion
accidentally spits out his drink. After gathering
himself.

"No mam I have my whole live ahead of me. I am
going to college and having kids are not on my list!"

"Good answer, now can you teach this bigheaded
boy something over here."

"I am trying too. They both turn and look at
Damion. Still eating his sandwich, he looks up with
food in his mouth.

"What?"

"Boy, your mother told me about all those days
miss from school. You should be ashamed of yourself."

"What, I do go to school that was the past. I am a
change man now."

"Umm hmm, don't walk across that stage, you will
see what crazy really is. Mr. I am a change man."

"Is this, gang up on me day."

"No boy." She starts to look at him strange.

"Speaking of change, are you okay? "

"Yes, why do you ask?"

"I do not know, but something is not right with
you." She pokes him in my face.

"Your whole aura is wrong."

"Okay, are you okay?" She sits back down.

"That is the oddest thing."

"Umm…what grandma?" She shakes her head.

"Never mind I guess I am a little tired. I need you to stay in school and go on to college, because there is nothing out here."

"I will grandma, but today is today and graduation is months away. I will worry about tomorrow.

"Tomorrow, well I do understand what it means to live for today, I am not that old. The issue is sometimes tomorrow never coming."

"Never comes, I'm not understanding."

"Are you slow? See life is a constant flow like how a river flows, and we all have different paths on this river. You can call it destiny or fate I prefer to call it God's divine plan. For example, point A is our start and your journey is to get to point J. However, in life we rarely take a straight line to our destination. We take alternating paths maybe a left we will call it point B or a right at point C or vice versa. Sometimes we make mistakes maybe we should have taken point C instead of B. However, that's usually in hindsight. Then there is times when we are stuck at a fix point in time. Sometimes in life you even get a do over"

"A do over." Damion looks at his grandmother strange.

"Yes, it is rare, however, does exist. It is when a mistake is made, and you are given a second chance to correct it."

"So, what if you do not correct the mistake you make?"

"That my son could be call, hell stuck doing the same thing repeatedly."

"Sounds more like insanity or deja vu." Kayla interjects.

"That sounds more like purgatory. You know the place between heaven and hell the final purification."

"Are you referring to the poem Inferno by Dante Alighieri?" Kayla looks at him.

"Don't look so surprise I am highly intelligent besides he was a poet and I like his name how can I not know about him." He starts to grin.

"You surprises me every day." Kayla begins to smile.

"Girl that makes two of us let me go and check on the rest of this food." The phone rings and Damion gets up and answered it.

"Hello."

"Aye D, we'll be there in about ten minutes."

"Cool, holla at you when you get here. Soon as he hangs up the phone. He is startle by his grandfather staring at him.

"Boy, who told you to answer my phone?"

"Gramps really."

"Yes really, boy let me tell you something. Do you pay the phone bill here?"

"No"

"What you say? I can't hear you. He places his hand by his ear.

I am not supposed to answer the phone sir."

"Then do not answer my phone then." Damion starts to get a little frustrated.

"Let us go, get your jacket babe. That was Devan they are on their way. Grandma we about to leave." She comes out the kitchen.

So soon, you just got here. Do not let your grandfather run you out of here. You know I do not pay that old man no attention."

"I heard that." Damion grandfather yells.

"No, it is not that my ride is on their way."

"Well let me walk you kids outside then."

Soon as they step outside of the door, Damion see Devan and Aliyah pulling up.

"Okay grandma I will call you when I get home.

"Okay baby, I love you."

"I love you too."

"Bye Miss Jones, I had a wonderful time it was a pleasure to meet you."

"No, the pleasure was all mine. You had better hold on to this one."

"Hey Grandma Jones." Devan yells out.

"Hello demon seed I mean Devan. You all get some safe. We drove off; Kayla looks at Damion that was interesting.

"Yeah, a little strange though she was beginning to sound like my mother."

"I don't know about that, but I like your grandmother."

"Yeah, she is cool like that she always had my back no matter what."

"So, what do you have plan for today?"

"Nothing other than work. I have to go home to get my uniform." Damion started laughing.

"You have to go to work and sell those jeepers.

"Whatever, I see you always got jokes. I am going to get you some for your birthday."

"You can keep those for yourself, but seriously what are you getting me it is only a few days away?"

"What do you want?"

"You know what I want?"

"You are not ready for this." She lays back in the corner of the seat.

"What, stop playing?" He begins to lean in and unzip her jacket and then her sweat top. She looks at the front seat then at Damion. He puts his hand under her shirt and starts rub and caress her breast. He can feel her heart racing as he starts to kiss her.

"Wait, not here." She repeatedly whispers. He pulls back.

"Okay I hear you." She sits back up and clear her throat while she zip her top and jacket back up.

"A Devan."

"Yeah." He turns down the go-go music that's playing.

"Can you drop us off over Kayla house, she lives over on Lang Place."

"Cool, we are almost there anyway. He turns the volume back up.

Everyone starts to sing along with the chorus, Do You Know What Time it is? (Tell me do you know?) Put your Gucci watch on synchronize the time and let's rock.

All the Time in the World

"Hey, I was thinking would you like to go to the prom with me? Kayla starts to laugh.

"What's so funny?

"You do know the prom is consider a school thing right."

"Oh, you are trying to be funny. Stop it, there is only one person funny in this relationship. Keep it up don't forget you want me to go to yours."

"You don't have to go I am sure I can find someone suitable. That won't mind going with all of this."

"That's cool, it would be the last prom you would ever attend though, but it is cool."

"Is that right, are you threatening me?"

"I don't do threats I just kick the truth to the young black youth."

"Okay we will see. He smiles.

"You sure about that?"

"I am positive. Are you?"

"We are here." They give each other some dap.

"All right dog I holla at you later. Bye Aliyah.

"Bye boy and bye Kayla."

"Bye, it was nice to meet you and I hope we can do it again. I got your number." Kayla opens her door to her house. They stood there in the living room.

"You gave Bonnie, I mean Aliyah your number? I don't like the way that sounds, my girl and a psycho talking."

"Yeah, she is sweet I don't see what the fuss is all about.

"Sweet yeah if you like mixing sugar with rat poison. Enough of that." He looks around the living room.

"Where are your parents?"

"You know they are not here, or you wouldn't be in here." Damion steps a little closer.

"I like the sound of that."

"Down boy. She puts her hand on his chest and stops him.

"What this, you want me to stop?

'You know I need to get dress and my parents will be home shortly." He leans towards her kisses her. They begin to kiss passionately until she breaks away from him, panting excessively.

"No baby I have to get dress." He instantly becomes irritated. He thought to himself, *you are playing with my emotion.*

"So, what was that all about earlier then?"

"What are you talking about?"

"What I'm talking about? You know what, never mind." He throws both his hands up.

"Whatever man."

"Whatever man?" She starts to get a little angry.

"Do you need me to walk you to your job?"

"No, my mother taking me and picking me up." He started walking towards the front door.

"What's the matter with you?"

"Nothing I can't handle. Well let me go. I do not want to further distract you from getting dress.

"Whatever, now you have a fucking attitude. You mad because you cannot get your way."

"I thought you had to get dress."

"So, it is like that?" He takes a deep sigh.

"Typical nigga don't get his way he act like an ass."

"Whatever this ass will holla at you later." He opens her door.

"What you holla, you are full of shit, you not going to say bye?"

"Bye baby you have a nice night." He closes the door behind him. He thought to himself, *I know she is piss now. Serves her right for messing with my emotions. Getting me all work up.* Meanwhile Kayla is stomping up her steps.

"That mother fucker just piss me off, I know did that shit on purpose he make me sick. Wait till I call his ass." Walking up the street towards his house, he was still thinking, *I hope she don't think I am going answer the phone when she calls because I don't feel like hearing that shit. Besides, I am getting into some shit tonight.* He starts to sing, Mad Word by Tears for Fears. Hide my head I want to drown my sorrow no tomorrow no tomorrow. The dreams in which I am dying are the best I have ever had. He started thinking, *where that came from; I must have heard it earlier.* Soon as he get in the house, he hears his phone ringing.

"Oh, hell I am not answering that. The phone rings repeatedly. He answers it.

"Hello." It was his job calling, asking him if he wanted to come in tonight. He tells them yeah, he will come in. He notice everyone was home except Big C. His sister was in the kitchen cooking dinner he tells her he is going to hop in the shower because he is going to work. While getting dress, he starts to listen to his sisters. They had him laughing out loud, kids say the craziest things they were playing house. Damion phone starts to ring again. He tells them he is out, and he's going to work at Shoe City. Damion love going to work. He would do it for free. Buying and selling shoes, flirting with the girls was his favorite pastime. His boy Darnell work there too. He went to Eastern also; however, their friendship started off in the oddest of ways. They went to the same infamous

Brown junior high together. Infect they were in the same homeroom. He could not stand Darnell he thought he was too much of a nerd. While they were in Eastern Damion had this crush on this girl who lived across the street from him name Ava. Everyone did though she was bad, she had this exotic look about her. However, he always thought she was out of his league. This was a brief time before Eva and him. One night when everyone was chilling outside on her side of the street. They all were having a good time listening to some music. He observers her getting out of a truck. He started thinking, *you got this boy.* He was already jive like feeling himself. Good job pockets on swollen and the girls are loving him too. He can't lose. Ava walks other to them, everyone speaks.

"Oh, you are chilling with us tonight."

"Boy don't look so surprise."

"I'm just saying." She interrupts him.

"Don't start nothing, it won't be nothing." Fats and Ava kept going back and forth. Damion walk ups to her.

"Hey Ava."

"Hey D."

"Can I holla at you for a second?"

"Sure, I am done talking to Mr. Know it all."

"I just wanted to let you know that I've been digging you for a while now. I don't know if you ever notice. All I know is right now I'm feeling your whole entire vibe."

"Honestly no, I had no idea you rarely speak to me other than the few times you came over to talk to my brother. I didn't think you even notice me." She blushes and smile.

Meanwhile Fats is taking bets on if Damion can close the deal or not. He put his money on him though. He was thinking, *damn she is on some humble type of shit. I didn't expect that.* He begins to smile.

Oh, so you notice me." She smiles back.

"There you go putting words in my mouth."

"Well instead of words how about numbers as in your phone number."

"You think you cute let me find out." She gives him her number and leaves. Of course, you know he was up in Fats face.

"I am a pimp there's no other words to describe me baby."

"This nigga swear he is a mac." Everyone starts laughing.

"However, pimp, she did just get out of somebody's truck."

"What are you driving?"

"Your mama's black Cadillac." While he was collecting his winnings, Fats tell him, oh you want to crack jokes. They go back and forth all night. A couple of days go by he and Ava are talking like crazy, he was really feeling shorty. One day at school he meets up with Black. He tells him about Ava.

"Word that is interesting, you know she messes with Darnell."

"Darnell who? What, stop playing?"

"You know who I'm talking about, your old classmate."

"The nerd from junior high?"

"He's not a nerd anymore he's out there in them streets now. Putting in work, running with them boys over there in Trinidad."

"Damn I just can't picture them two being together."

"Yeah infect they been together for a couple of years."

"Man get the fuck out of here I know you are playing now."

"Nah I am serious for real I'm surprise you didn't know that. That's his truck she be getting out of."

"Damn, was shorty trying to play me? Okay I appreciate the info dog." They give each other some dap.

"I will holla at you later." Damion was going to see shorty regardless he was practically over her house every night getting his freak on. He thought, *hell she wasn't going to mention him, you damn for sure know I wasn't.*

One day Black tells Damion that Darnell knows something is up with old girl and him.

"Oh yeah, I was wondering why all the sudden he has been staring towards my direction. How did he even find out about us anyway?"

"Hey, I don't know. What you going to do? "

"The same shit I have been doing that nigga is not suicidal."

"I know that's right. Black begins to laugh. Time goes by and he starts to see this dude truck a lot more. One night he calls her and ask her what is up with her boy Damon?

"Nothing, where just friends, we use to fool around back in the day

"Back in the day huh."

"Yeah, back in the day.

Stop fucking lying to me trick! Well that is what Damion was thinking to himself. He like her a lot, but he knew that she wasn't his girl. That's why he couldn't understand what was all the lying for. The weirdest thing happen one day Damion was out looking for a job because his mother was on her throwing him out mood again. He went into Shoe City that day looking for the 995 New Balances because everywhere else they were sole out. He left out of there with a new job.

His first day on the job the manager tells him she is going to introduce him to a co-worker that will show him the ropes. He walks in the room and see

Darnell I thought, *isn't this a bitch.* It was awkward as hell at first. However, the funniest thing happened as they gotten to know each other, the tighter they became. In fact, they became such good friends they hung out all the time going on double dates. Not with Ava though with other girls. By this time, Damion was feeling a little guilty. Even though he knew Darnell was dating other girls. He knew that Ava was his main one. So, he faded back. He stay silent when they use to go over Ava house together. The first time they went over there together. It felt weird to him, he couldn't believe he went with him, but he did. He probably went because he was a little curious, besides he was always playing with someone head. He just wanted to see her face. They were all over there looking stupid. Sitting on the couch, barely any conversation was going on between them. Awkward to say the least especially when they were all sitting on the couch. The same couch were he and she laid on doing their thing. She just sat there looking discomfort. That was Damion first taste of a lying ass scant with a pretty face. He just sat there *thinking all that time you was lying. It was all for what though.* He just stop talking to her all together. Shaking his head, he thought, *pretty faces are going to be the death of him.* Darnell and he never spoke of it, and he never told him that they were sharing the same girl. That is how it all started, talk about irony.

The whole gang was there tonight Damion, Darnell, Catarina, Imani and our cool as assistant manager Justen. They all shared a radio there that they would play their tapes, if there were no cuss words in it. Everyone would have his or her tapes ready to play. Poison by BBD was playing at the time.

"Did Justin call you in?" Darnell ask Damion.

"You know it."

"And you came?"

"Man, I love this joint I was not doing anything anyway."

"Where is Catarina anyway?"

"She is around here somewhere probably upstairs. Do you two still talk?

"Hell no! She has too many issues, probably because of all the mix breeding. She needs an exorcist a priest a rabbi and then some." See Catarina was cool as hell, but she had too many problems. She came from a big as family she was mix Black, Brazilian and Italian and she act like all of them. She and Damion went out a few times and he did not know whom he was talking to half of time. She was probably the most beautiful girl he had ever dated in his young life. She had a body like no other and a Red bone which was his weakness. It was an addiction he couldn't seem to stop. Damion goes upstairs looking to unload some boxes.

"Hey D, I didn't know you were working today?"

"Oh hey, Catarina I didn't see you over there. Yeah, they ask me to come."

"So, what have you been up too?"

"You know me same old same." You never got back with me about us switching next week for my birthday."

"That's cool and all but what are you going to do for me?"

"Umm—what do you mean?"

"Do you not understand the words that are coming from out of my mouth?

"Yeah, so what do you want?"

"Eu sei que você émedo de mim. (I know you fear me.) I will let you know. Then she smacks him on the butt. She walks back down the steps. He shakes his head he already knows this is going to be trouble. After putting the boxes and clothes up. Justin tells Damion he needs him back on the floor. He started to go back downstairs when he heard noises. At least he thought he did. He took a step back and look around. Nothing but silence, so he walk back downstairs. The store was getting very crowded; Damion ask Darnell where all these people come from.

"Beats me it got like this soon as you went upstairs. So, what is up with you and your girl?"

Who?"

"Catarina, you know who." He starts to grin.

"Don't you mean your girl?"

"Not, nah and no. That chic have multiple personalities."

"Tell me about it, she was going on me earlier then started acting all nice and shit like nothing happen." Imani comes over and interrupted them.

"Are you going to help or BS the rest of the night?"

"Girl shut your flat ass up we are working."

"Hey, my butt is not flat." She turns to the side to look at it.

"You sure fool me pancake girl."

"You are just jealous because you want what you cannot have."

"Darnell interrupts; you almost made me throw up in my mouth." Damion started laughing.

"Ooh, you two make me sick." She rolled her eyes and walk towards the back. Justin pulls me to the side.

"Hey playa let me talk to you for a second."

"Oh okay, what's up?"

"Catarina fine big ass." He looks at Justin strangely.

"Look, here I know you two have been out on a few dates before. Just give me the 411. Damion started laughing.

"Are you serious?"

"Hell, yeah, she is always flirting with me calling me sexy. That girl be having my temperature rising. I need another baby mama."

"That is what she always do. She is a big flirt. Do not do it I am trying to warn you. Don't trust a big butt and a smile.

"Then warn me because I am a glutton for punishment. Holla at her for me and see what's up."

"Do what? He stop and thought about it. Okay but it is going to cost you."

"I don't care how much it cost whatever it takes just do it. Catarina comes out from the back.

"What did you two say to Pancake?"

"Man, she'll be alright."

"I know it was you D you are always fucking around."

"Me does it always have to be me?"

"Because it's always is."

"Hold that thought for a second, I need to help this young woman over there." It was getting close to closing time and they were listening to the radio when 911 is a Joke comes on by Public Enemy. Followed by Mama Said Knock You Out by LL Cool J. That is when everyone really started to mess around with each other especially when all the customers left out of the store. Damion kept thinking to himself, *I need to call, Fats and see what they are trying to do tonight.* He finally gets a chance to call him.

"What up fool?"

"Moms wanted me to call her to see what's up with tonight. She told me pops is not laying it down like he use too. She told me I could stop in from time to time. You know like a designated hitter." Because we fuck with you each other real tuff, you don't even have to call me daddy. We just going to keep it between us two, you know keep it on the hush."

"Shit I just came from your mother apartment where she down there washing my underwear and cooking my dinner. She wanted to say thank you in her own special way."

"Now that is just nasty, what are you doing tonight?"

"I don't know yet, but we are getting into something though. What time are you getting off?" "Around 9:00."

"We are coming to pick you up."

"Who is we?"

"Lowell and I."

"That will work I don't feel like staying in tonight. After hanging up the phone.

"What are you getting into tonight?" Darnell ask. Fats is coming to get me."

"Man, I am taking my black ass home I am in for the night you know school is tomorrow. He looks at Damion. He tried hard not to laugh.

"I am not even going to ask because I already know the answer."

"Friday is part of the weekend that means no school. I will be back Monday.

"What is you doing for your birthday?

"I don't know, but I can't worry about tomorrow when today isn't here. Besides, I'll get that much needed sleep when I am dead."

"I hear you. Help me with the door.

"Okay I will get the chains its lock down time.

"About time you are doing some work. Imani yells.

"Work these, Pancake."

"Somebody needs to do something about your mouth.

"Hey maybe it will be the same person that is going to do something about your butt." Darnell starts to grin; she just stood there looking at Damon. He felt bad, so he stop laughing.

"Man do not pay her any attention, laugh that shit up she just mad. She always doing that. She is always messing with us. She is always snitching on us, like she's the teacher's pet." Ac purple of minutes passes by. Darnell comes from behind the counter.

"Hey, I just got off the phone with Ava she want me to bring her something to eat, so I am going that way if you need a ride?"

"Okay let me call Fats. I knew your fat ass haven't left yet. After talking to Fats, he tells Darnell just drop him off at the house.

"Let's roll then dog."

"Cool just have to make a stop to get something to eat."

"I can change when I get home. Finally, they were off and driving, after stopping and getting something to eat. Damion was staring at the windshield.

"You okay my nigga?"

"Oh yeah, I'm straight I was thinking about something that happen earlier today. What Damion was really thinking about, *was this infamous truck park across the street all the time. Irony can be funny at times.*

"Hey, my man throwing this house party this weekend. Let me know if you're trying to roll?"

"Sounds like a plan, you know I will"

"What time it starts?"

"Everything kicks off at 8:00"

"My man that's what I'm talking about. Do I need to bring anything?

"Nope everything is going to be right there, the drinks the weed. Like I said everything."

"It's been one long as day. Damion turns on the radio and BabyFace is playing he changes the station saying out loud, nope I don't want to hear that. As he goes through each station. Mad World was playing. He thought that is oddest thing, *how he keep hearing this song for some reason.*

"What's that Tears for Fears? Darnell ask.

"What you know about them young buck?"

"What are you talking about, they use to play their videos all the time on Friday Night Videos."

"Damn I forgot all about that show. Does it still come on?"

"Who know Tears for Fears huh? About the same time, they broke out singing Shout, Shout let it all out these are the things I can do without come on I'm talking to you come on.

"That's some funny as shit. Man, that was the song."

"Yeah just thinking what I need for Saturday. Shit I forgot we got a football game early that day.

"With who?"

"Who knows, I never do it's with someone though. I am not trying to stay in the house this weekend. I hate being bored."

"I know it is too much shit to get into. Who wants to be coop up in the house?"

"Just been having this feeling lately that I need to do something and not the same old thing neither." They pull up to Damion's building.

"Okay dog, you know I appreciate the ride."

"No problem slim see you Saturday.

"No doubt, holla."

"Holla." He and Damion dap up. He gets out of the truck and started walking when a thought pop into his head what if the joke was really on him. He knew Darnell was connected to some powerful people. Only after becoming close friends. However, what if he was just keeping his circle tight. You know that old saying; keep your friends close and your enemies closer. Damion look back for a second, nah I think I let my imagination get the better of me sometimes.

The Beginning of the End

He looks up and almost run into Keisha and his sister. They were talking in the hallway. He notices his sister looking all teary up.

"What is wrong with you?"

"Nothing, I will call you later Keisha. My sister walks back downstairs into the house.

He looks at Keisha.

"Why are you staring at me?"

"What is going with my sister? What did you do?"

"What did I do to Amani?" Damion steps closer to Keisha.

"Yeah, you heard me. What did you do, she looks like she been crying?

So, the first thing that comes to your mind is I did something. I mean umm. She interrupts him while clapping her hand.

"Yes, please tell me what you mean?"

There is no need for all that animated crap you are doing. Hey, I am just trying to find out what's up."

"Then you need to ask your sister then and stop interrogating me like you the police."

"You know what why is it every time I talk to you it feels like it's a heavy weight fight."

"That sounds like a personal problem."

"It is more like you're my problem."

"I am not your problem. You do not have to worry about that."

"Always with the answers, huh? Don't act like I don't know you."

"First of all, you don't know everything you think you do; you just play that role well baby."

"My role huh, you funny as hell, matter of fact where's Kathy at I need her to explain my role to you. Keisha begin to grin, leave my mother out of this. She steps even closer to Damion, almost to the point of kissing. With a smile on her face tells him.

"What's the matter did I hurt your feelings or something huh? You only crack jokes when you're trying to cover up a pain of yours. Don't forget I know you too." She blows a kiss then sidesteps him and walks out of the hallway. He just stood there for a second; "I wish you was a dude, just once. Damn, she got me again, I have to be quicker than that." Mumbling to himself, he see his sister sitting at the table drinking something.

"What's wrong sis? Before she could answer. What's his name and what did he do?" She looks up at him

"What are you talking about? I'm just going through something."

"So, when did we start keeping secrets from one another?"

"I just do not want to talk about it right now."

"You know you can always come and talk to me that is what big brothers are for. You having problems at school with some bama? Please let it be that punk ass boyfriend of yours. You know I do not like him anyway; I should fuck him up just for general purpose."

"No and the rest of that you're talking stop. Because lately never mind."

"Never mind, lately, what does that supposed to mean?"

You are never here anyway you are always with Fats or them other bozos. Or you are at work."

"It is not always like that sometimes I am with my girl too. I'm just messing with you

"I forgot about the big headed one. She says under her breath.

"What?"

"Oh nothing."

"Umm hmm, yeah right."

"What's up with you and Keisha?"

There will be no mention of the Native American girl from the tribe of Never Hoe to me. He becomes very agitated as he sits in the chair.

"Don't you mean Navajo, as in Navajo Indians?"

"Girl I know what I said. She is a Never Hoe. They were lost in the Appalachian Mountains many moons ago." She couldn't help but to laugh.

Something is definitely wrong with you. What is it now, you two get into it again? He walks into the bathroom

"If you want to call it that."

"Sound more like foreplay to me." She says under her breath."

"What?"

"I didn't say anything."

"All I know is she always got something to say about everything."

"Boy you aren't bright at all are you?"

"Bright, what are you talking about now?

"Oh nothing. She just shakes her head. He sticks his head out of the bathroom door.

"Are you okay?"

"Yes, I am."

"Well when you are ready to talk just let me know."

"Okay I will when I'm ready. I don't know when you're clueless in your own life. She once again says under breath.

"Hey, I will make it to you I promise. You know I love you right?"

"Yes, I know."

"Well I'm gone, don't wait up I will talk to you later." The door closes behind him and she just sits there staring with a blank expression on her face. With a tear slowly rolling down here cheek.

"I love you too." Upstairs knocking on Fats door Deon answer it.

"What are you doing up here, are you rolling with us?"

"Hell no, just talking to your boy for a minute." Damion sits on the couch and begins to look for the remote for the television.

"So, what are you up to tonight?"

"Going over this new honey dip spot, I pull a couple of weeks ago."

"What the hell is a honey dip anyway?"

"You need to stay fresh with the lingo youngster." Fats comes out of the kitchen eating a sandwich.

"I figured you would be in there. Do you ever get tire of stuffing your face?"

"Do you ever stop and think and say to yourself I do have a big mouth. Just once I should shut the fuck up."

"Nope, the thought never cross my mind. So, where are the parents tonight?"

"That's on a need to know basic and you don't need to know."

"I think you need to finish eating your sandwich because you keep talking like you got your panties in a bunch. Man are we rolling or what?"

"Chill out we are waiting on Lowell he just got off work."

"Finally, the remote. He turns the television on. It was straight to his show, The Box.

"Its video time."

"No, it's not." And proceeds to grab the remote and turn the television off.

"What gives?"

"What gives? I tell you what gives, how about you ask first."

"May I watch The Box on your television?"

"No!"

"You know you got mayonnaise all over your pants." He looks down.

"Damn it." He walks toward his bedroom.

"Box time. He turns the television back on.

"You are addictive to this crap."

"Yup and mind your business." The video Smooth Operator by Sade was on.

You know something, I was never really into Sade like that, but she jive like sexy as hell though.

"What you know about that young blood that's grown folk's music right there."

"I don't know all about that, but I do know sexy. Speaking of sexy do I know this so call honey dip of yours?"

"Nah but she is friends, with–damn I forgot her name she use to live next door to you.

"I know you're not talking about—damn what is her name?"

"Oh, it's Helena."

"Oh, she is friends with Hoeleena." Deon looks at Damion surprise.

"Oh yeah, I forgot that's what everybody use to call her."

"Yeah, she was fake as hell with her want to be uppity ass. Turn out she was giving ass away like bean pies. So, she's friends with Hoeleena. Is she a hoe too? As Deon puts his drink back down.

"Yeah, basically."

"What is that you're drinking anyway?"

"This is some new shit called Sysco."

"I heard of it. It looks like a wine cooler?" He starts grinning.

"Yeah something like that, go ahead and try some. See if you like it."

"Sounds like a setup to me. Okay, I will bite. He drinks some.

"What crack of ass was that made from?" My chest is burning."

"You didn't like it?"

"I mean it had a sweet refreshing taste to it. Hell no, I didn't like it. That cannot be a wine cooler."

"Oh yeah, I forgot to tell you they call it liquid crack. Damion wipes his mouth.

"Liquid crack, why would anyone want to drink that?" The phone begins to ring. I

"Your phone is ringing!"

"No shit Sherlock!" Fats yell back

"Everyone wants to be an asshole. I beginning to think it's a disease."

"I see and you're the first one standing in line. Fats come's back into the living room

"That was Lowell he's going to meet us at the car." They all leave out and started walking towards the car. Damion starts to get feel a cold chill going down his spine.

"You feel that?"

"Feel what?"

"Feel what, that cold as breeze.

"Boy there is no breeze out here tonight."

"That's just that ghost dancing on your soul." Deon tells him

"Ha, whatever you say cuz, besides I am the only good one out here anyway. I'm not worried about my soul. However, you might need to worry about yours." Fats intervenes.

"I know you're not talking about anyone soul."

"Didn't you just steal Melvin in the face for nothing last week."

"Oh, that was different."

"Different how?"

"Yeah different like you know I was defending my sister honor."

"What you think this is the Wide Wild West?"

"Nah, it is DC baby much worst. Besides ain't no one scared of no ghost. Now zombies that something different. I don't fuck with them at all."

"You dumb as shit talking about zombies if you wasn't my cousin."

"All I'm saying is I don't fuck with them. They all get in the car except Deon he's on the passenger side talking to Lowell.

"Okay I got an example for you.

"Here we go."

"Nah, man just listen. Okay we all know how these crack heads be out here feining right. Two guys walk up from out of Keisha building. They look familiar, but no one knew them. They did know Deon. He stop and turned around when they spoke to him. Shortly after speaking, they got into a white Lexus ES 300 in front of us. Okay as I was saying there was this new Jamaican product that came into the hood that was so potent it had everyone going mad crazy over it." Deon interrupts the story.

"Man, I got that shit now. Everyone starts laughing.

"Man, ain't nobody talking about that baking soda down crap you be selling."

"You better ask somebody." Fats interrupts Damion.

"How long is this story?"

"If you don't stop interrupting me, I could finish. Anyway, like I was saying before I was rudely interrupted. They all started to go mad crazy. This new product called Voodoo, was driving people insane. They started to attack the drug dealers looking for more drugs. Then the drug dealers started beating and shooting at them. It all became hopeless because they couldn't seem to stop them. The crack heads begin to overwhelm them. The need for Voodoo overwhelm their basic need for everything, like food, water…etc. One by one the drug dealers begin to disappear. Next thing you know people in general were beginning to disappear. The drug dealers and what was left of the community band together to stop the killing spree. Unbeknownst to them was that the Voodoo carried some type of infectious disease. Once it enter your bloodstream it takes over your blood then your heart and finally your brain. They became an unstoppable monster. Even when they would get hurt, mane, dismember, or shot they would keep coming after you because the drug was taking over their mind. And the only way you can stop them is to cause major damage to their heads like shooting them in it. There it is fellas the crack head zombie apocalypse. It was complete silence in the car until Fats says.

"Get the fuck out here." They all begin to laugh.

"I'm just saying that joint sounds like a movie of the week. I don't know what you're talking about. I need to write that one down."

"Yeah you do that. Fats replied.

"So how does it end?"

"How does what end?"

"You know the story." All eyes are on Damion with anticipation. In a condescending voice.

"Oh, now you want to hear the rest of my story. That's when he notice out the corner of his eye a car coming up the street moving slowly. He thought to himself that's odd. He tried to get a better look, but he really couldn't see because the lights on that side of the street where always out. The car stop. That's when everything started to move in slow motion. Deon was calling his cousin name repeatedly.

"Are you going to finish your story?"

"I'm not thinking about them zombies." They all begin to laugh all over again. Damion looks at Deon. That's when he hears the screeching sound of tires colliding with the cold asphalt.

"Oh shit!" Damion yells as he goes back seat diving. On the way down he see his cousin diving to the ground; Fats yelling give me my gun. Endless rounds were firing, one after another. Shortly afterwards you could hear two separate car tires screeching as they drove away. Deon jumps up and start firing back, but they were already too far gone. Deon started checking himself.

"Is everyone okay? "They all get out of the car yeah, we are okay. Deon ask me you okay yeah you know it's not my first rodeo. Fats started walking around the car.

"What the hell was that about? I don't see any holes in the car.

"Where they even shooting at us?" Damion asks.

"Either they were shooting at Jay or they're literally the worst shooters ever. Spray and pray as I guess. There is nothing but smoke, and the smell of lead and burnt tires in the air. No one seemed to know anything.

"Here comes the sirens late as usual. It's time to go." Deon yells. Everyone jump in their car and rolled out. Damion just sits back and takes a deep breath, and thought, *it's just another day on my street.* It was so quiet you could hear a pen drop. Damion expression on his face was of a sadden one.

"What's wrong?" Lowell ask.

"I didn't know Fats was that flexible and could bend that low." They all started laughing;

"I know you're not talking you were in the drowning in the backseat."

"Whatever, I don't know what you're talking about."

Just another crazy night in the neighborhood, so where are we going? I am not trying to go to those places that you like frequent all the time either Fats. A Lowell, where are we going since Fats cannot seem to find his voice?"

"Where going wherever life takes us."

"Okay Dalai Lama I see already this is going to be a long night."

Deon World

It is 12:04 am Friday the 16th. Deon just left the fellas and is on his way to his girl Tameka apartment. She lives in the Paradise apartments off Minnesota Avenue. Deon hears the subtle sounds of reggae music in the background. He puts his ear against the door. He thinks *that is where the music is coming from.* He pauses before he knocks, he checks the handgun concealed in his pants behind his lower back. He begins to knock on the door. Tameka opens the door wearing a wife beater and booty shorts on. He walks in as he greets her.

"Well hello there."

"Hey, baby." She grabs his hand and leads him to the couch. His thoughts were of gratification as he looks at that booty moving left to right. He thought, *damn she's phat as shit, this is going to be a good night.* He sat down and notice the entire coffee table was covered with weed.

"What is this the weed house?" She grins as she sits on his lap and straddle him

Don't worry yourself about that." She begins to kiss him and grab his hands and put them on her butt. They begin to kiss more; Deon thinks he heard a noise. He thought to himself, *am I am tripping.* Then he hears the sound again.

"What was that?"

"What was what?"

"I heard something, is someone else in here?

"Oh, that is probably—before she could finish a girl walks out from the room. Deon push his Tameka to the side and pull his gun.

"Oh shit!" She yells as she jump back behind the wall.

"Baby I was trying to tell you; I have a roommate. Andria you can come out now. Can you put your gun away now, you are scaring my girl?"

"My fault." He puts his gun away.

"Come here baby." Andria comes out from behind the wall with a lit up white boy. She takes a couple of puffs as she walks over towards the couch. Deon started thinking to himself; *damn she is thicker than Tameka.* Wearing a used jeans denim shirt with booty shorts and thigh high socks on. She and Tameka started doing shotguns. They gave the white boy to Deon, as he begins to smoke, they started kissing each other. Deon thought to himself, *yeah this is going to be a great night.* Then Andria leans in and started doing shotguns with Deon. Shortly afterwards they begin to kiss as well. Tameka begin to unzip Deon pants as they position themselves on opposite's side of each other. They started to go down on him while he was still smoking his white boy. He thought to himself, *if only he had a handheld camera that could record all of this. I would be a legend.* The cloud of weed smoke was thick in the air and it had them hype more than usual. Next thing Deon knew, the girls got up and started dancing. Tameka turns the stereo up louder, as Andria started dancing harder. Tameka tells Deon Andria puts that A in ass. Andria drops down to the floor shaking her booty to the song Daddy's Little Girl by Nikki D. She put on a show as Deon observe her skill set.

"I am hungry, is anyone else?"

"I'm starving too". Andria answers. So, they whip something up in the kitchen. He smacks her on the butt.

"Ooh you know how I like it daddy." She comes back with some shot glasses and a liter of Hennessy. It was shot after shot after shot.

"Finish up I am needed in the kitchen." She cleaned the table and brought the food out.

"Dinner is served." They all sat at table and eat.

"Damn, you can cook too."

"What is all of this?"

"Curry chicken, brown rice, beans rolls cabbage and spinach." After they finish eating and drinking.

They both took Deon by the hand and led him to Tameka's bedroom to finish the threesome they started. The girls started kissing each other and then they took turns kissing him.

"We share everything in this household.

"Well I don't want to disrupt the household traditions. I am down with that. Besides, I heard sharing is caring."

"Then you my friend are in luck." The night was long and so was the passion that was brewing. They all took turns pleasuring themselves. The lines became intertwine and sex became an expression of exhibitionism. Deon woke up next to Tameka and Andria spooning each other he smiles and gets dress. He looks at the clock on the wall shit it is 3:00. He walks into the living room to get his jacket off the couch. When he notice all the weed left on the table in bags. He thought to himself, *I don't think they need all of this weed I'll just help myself to a little.* He finally gets to his car and drives off.

He drove to a Seven Eleven, to get something to drink. He pulls in and park. After walking into the store to get a bottle of water he notice two police officers were standing not too far behind him. He thought to himself, *where in the hell did, they come from I didn't see any police cars outside.* He turn to his left and notice one of them was staring at him. *Be cool Deon they have nothing on you.* He thought.

"Hey, can I get a Jamaican beef patty?" He starts to feel the presents of one of the officers standing directly behind him. The dude at the register was in a dazed.

"Hello, did you hear me?"

"I am sorry what did you want again sir?"

"Two beef patties."

"Mild or spicy?"

"Spicy please." He gives him the patties and Deon gives him the money and leaves out. But before doing so he look up at the mirror on the wall and saw them both staring at him. He couldn't get to his car quick enough. He open the car door and that's when the contact hit him. He thought damn this car smell like pure weed. He started smelling himself oh shit I smell like weed that's when it dawns on him as he look back at the store. It's time for me to get the hell out of dodge. While he was driving, he crack his windows and turn on the radio Deja vu by Teena Marie was playing. Followed by Young love by Teena Marie. Finally, he's home. After barely reaching the top of the stairs, Deon collapse in his bed. He wakes up to loud music playing outside.

"What the hell is going on? Who is playing that? Who the fuck is driving this early in the morning? What is that, is that Tears for Fears." He looks at the clock on the wall. Damn it's going to be hard as hell trying to get back to sleep now.

Friday the 16, 8:00 am. Deon wakes up to an unfamiliar sound. Muscle memory makes him reach for his gun. He thinks, *wait a minute, where am I?* He looks around the room and see the posters on the wall. *How in the hell did I get here?* He begins to look at himself. That's when he looks up and see his sister standing in the doorway.

"You're not in the Twilight zone, just in the wrong apartment idiot." She shakes her head and walks away. She comes back.

"Oh, I forgot to tell you mom made breakfast and she wants you to come down and get something to eat before she leaves for work."

"What time is it?"

"It is a little after 8:00, are you okay your eyes look bloodshot."

"Yeah, I'm fine tell mom I will be down there in a minute.

"Do something to your eyes first." About fifteen minutes later Deon comes walking down the stairs.

"Hey mom."

"Good morning baby, did you have a rough night?"

"No, why you ask?"

"Well baby if you thought this was your apartment last night, I think there is something wrong son."
I know you love me. However, I do recall a certain

someone trying to break their neck to get their own place."

"Nah mom, it's not like that."

"Hush boy the lord always pushes trouble souls in the direction where they can get help even if they know it or not."

"You don't have to worry about me mom I can take care of myself."

"I know you can, that's not the point I am your mother I will always worry about you and your sister that is my job." She looks at her watch.

"Oh, I'm going to be late for work. Girl umm–a girl whatever your name is, you better come down here now and eat this food before it gets cold."

"Make sure your sister eats and lock up after she leaves. We will finish this conversation another time."

"Okay mom bye." She hugs him and walks out the door. Deon starts yelling.

"A girl, or whatever your name is you better come down here and eat this food before it gets cold. Peaches comes into the kitchen and grab a bacon and toast with one hand and takes a bite and walks over to Deon and sticks her fingers in his orange juice and lick her fingers.

"You happy now." She turns around and walks back upstairs.

"Has anyone ever told you that you are a sick individual?

"Yes, they do, and I tell them I learned it all from my big brother." He turns back around in his seat and ponder for a second; she might have a point with that one. Oh well there is no reason to cry over spilled milk. I need to finish this food before I go home. After eating Deon goes back upstairs to collect his weed. He see Peaches going into his old room.

"Why are you still here you better be going to school?"

"Just waiting on you so I can lock up."

Oh, okay I'm gone then. I will holla at you later girl.

Okay, whatever we will see. Maybe, if you do more pop ups in the middle of the night. Deon finally gets home and yells out home sweet home, I need to jump in the shower. After changing clothes, Deon made some phone calls to a few weed heads. He turns his television on and starts roll up a white boy to smoke. He took a couple of puffs of it when his phone starts to ring.

"What up, nigga I know you didn't play us like that."

"Who is this?" He tries to say with a straight face.

"You know who it is."

"Oh, my fault Tameka what's happening girl?" Deon starts coughing.

"I know you not smoking my shit."

"Girl I am coming down with a head cold."

"Oh, you on joke time I see. Well since you on joke time, I got a joke for you. What is it call, when you're burnt to a fucking crisp with their dick is jam down their throat?

"Damn that sounds like a chicken dinner."

"We know about your rep. that shit don't scare us. If you don't give our shit back with interest. That's your ass nigga."

"Bitch, who do you think you talking too?"

"Apparently, your bitch ass, nigga you done stole from the wrong people."

"Bitch, to know me and my rep, is to die by me. I want you to remember those words with ease.

"My niggas are going to fuck you up."

"First spell apparently second eat a dick up to you hiccup BITCH!" He slams the phone down so he can finish rolling and smoking his weed. He pulls his gun out.

"People do not seem to have any respect anymore. I see we are going to have to teach them all a lesson. Isn't that right honey. I need to stop messing with these tricks out here there are trying to turn me into something that I am not."

Lowell World

It is 6:04 am Friday 16th. The alarm goes off, the snooze button is hit. After a few times the alarm is finally, stop at 6:45. A Mad World is playing. Lowell finally gets up. His first thought *shit I am going to be late.* He jumps into the shower and gets dress. His girl Taylor was outside waiting in her car.

"I am sorry I'm late."

"I take it you had a rough night."

"No, I just didn't get enough sleep."

"I bet I know you wasn't home I tried to call you."

"I told you the fellas and me where going to hang out."

"How long was that, you know what never mind, I guess that's none of my business?"

"I didn't say that."

"Well, I stop to get you some breakfast and coffee."

"Thank you, babe, I knew there was something I like about you."

"Funny, I know…hold up don't eat all of it save me some greedy."

"Oh, my fault." Lowell turns on the radio to listen to 980 sports radio station.

"Are you going to be okay sweetie you look so tire your eyes are so red? You look like you been smoking all night. Wait a minute pass me my purse please I think I have some eye drops in here somewhere. Let me see, here we go I found it. Let me put a couple of drops in your eyes. Because you know, you have a straight up asshole for a supervisor."

"I know babe, you know I can handle Mr. Matthews." Lowell went back to listening to the radio.

"Umm sweetie…hello, I said hello." She turns and looks at Lowell. Nevertheless, there is still no response.

"She said sweetie again, are you listening to me?

"Umm hmm." Was all that she received.

"Oh really, okay I was watching television last night when a man kick in my door. He pick me up, took me to my bedroom. After throwing me down on the bed. I tried to fight him off, but he told me I am going to like it to I love it. You know what he was right I love every minute of it. He put me to sleep like no other. What you think of that?

"Umm hmm, I hear you."

"What, I knew you was not paying me any attention?"

"Baby I heard everything you said, keep playing with me with your man stories. That was a weak as nap you were taking about, I am going to put you in a comma. So, can I go back to listening to the radio now?"

"Oh, so I guess I need to shut up then."

"See we are on the same page.

"I know you did not just say that.

You know I am just playing with you. He started smiling. After finding a parking space in the underground garage, they work at. He leans in and kiss her. After a brief kiss, she stops him and looks around.

"Wait we are at work." Lowell gets out and slams the door. She sits back in her seat and takes a deep breath. They both work at a small marketing firm downtown but in separate departments. Taylor was in a higher department a lot higher up the cooperate ladder then Lowell was. He sat down for ten minutes with his head on his desk. When Mr. Matthews (aka Mr. Mass) walks in his cubicle. Everyone at work calls him because his breath smell like a monkey armpits and ass,

"Now, now, Mr. Reese sleeping on the job already, you know we do not tolerate that."

"I was not sleeping I have a headache; how may I help you Mr. Mass I mean Mr. Matthews?"

"Huh, what was that?"

"How may I help you sir?"

"Yes, you may, you can first start by not sleeping on my time." He steps closer to Lowell. Lowell moves back in his seat I need these reports taking care ASAP as he take two more steps closer to him. Lowell slowly takes another step back until he could not move anymore. Mr. Matthews leans in real close and drops a bigger folder into his lap.

"I want this report also done by noon today." Mr. Matthews continues to talk, and Lowell is starting to get a little lightheaded from his breath.

"Are you okay Mr. Reese you look like you are about to faint."

"I am fine sir."

"Well when you are finish, please stop by my office. You know it is evaluation time." With a devilish smile on his face he walks out of the cubicle. He finally let his breath out.

"Shit, my nose is burning. He starts to look around when he begins opening the folders.

"I am getting tire of this shit. He gets up and walk out of the cubicle and runs into a few of his coworkers.

"What did Mr. Mass want?"

"You know the same old shit, trying to inflict as much pain as he can with his breath."

"He has to know his breath stink, and that it repels all living creatures." One of the coworkers said out loud.

"Yes, he does it on purpose, all up in your personal space and shit." Lowell thought to himself, he *has one more time.*

"Okay folks I will talk to you all later I need to take care of some business." He started walking down the hall into the men's restroom. Let me see if anyone is in here. He takes the last stall. It's relaxing time, Lowell starts to fall asleep. When he hears a sound, *I know no one is in the next stall. What the fuck. You must be kidding me I know they are not breaking restroom etiquette. You do not sit next to someone in a stall unless there is no spaces left.* Then the smell and the noises ensued afterwards. He gets up and walk out of the stall and yell.

"It's seven empty fucking stalls in here and you are going to sit next to me. This is some bull shit." He walks out of there and finds another rest room on another floor and takes a nap. He even finish both reports with time to spare.

The phone rings Lowell answers.

"Hello." It was Taylor.

"Is everything okay, what's wrong?"

"Nothing is wrong, everything is peachy."

"You sure, why do you sound like that?"

"I am fine just finish a pile of work giving to me by my asshole of a supervisor."

"Do you still want to have lunch, or are you to tire?" He hesitated for a second.

"I am never to tire for you baby. Yes, I would love to have lunch with you today."

"Okay, because I need to talk to you."

"I am all yours."

"That is what I wanted to hear baby; I will call you back bye." She calls him back in thirty minutes. They both decided to eat in the cafeteria for lunch. Taylor ask him.

"Why do you look worst then you look this morning."

"I do not know it was a rough morning to say the least.

"How is your day going so far?"

"I am maintaining. They begin to talk about Mr. Matthews.

"What's is wrong with your boy?" Taylor ask.

"That is not my boy with his short ass." Her smiles begins to light up the room.

"Well I did want to talk to you." With a grin on his face, he stares at her.

"So, what do you want to talk to me about?" She reaches out and puts her hand on top of his.

"How long are we going to keep doing this? His smile quickly vanishes from off his lips.

"What are you talking about?"

"You know damn well, what I am talking about. I'm sorry I shouldn't have said it like that."

"What is going on with you? We were just talking about eating."

"Why are you doing this?"

"You are asking why I am doing this." He snatches his hand away and puts his fork down.

"So, this is where you want to do this?"

"Why are you getting so loud?" Everyone starts to lift his or her heads up. He lower his voice.

"You are the one, who wanted to do this here, not me."

"I thought we were having a good time. Enjoying each other company laughing and eating."

"Like I said, how long we are going to keep doing this? This talking but not talking." Lowell starts to scratch his head as he gets more and more frustrated.

"You move out of our apartment to help your brother out temporarily. However, it seems like is more than that. Most of your stuff is gone now. You barely even look at me let alone touch me."

"Here we go. I'm just trying to take care of my family."

"I thought I was part of your family."

"You are, and you know you are."

"What am I supposed to think?"

"Think what you want to think." She puts her hand on his arm I know you blame me for our daughter, before she could finish her sentence. He interrupts her.

"Don't you dare do this, get your hands off me."
He gets up and is visibly upset.

"What do you want from me?"

"I tell you what I want, I want your respect your love and above all else your loyalty."

"You know what you don't have to worry about me getting home I will walk before I get into that car with you." Taylor watches him slams his food in the trashcan as he walks away while her cheeks begin to feel wet and warm at the same time, from her tears. Lowell walks back towards his cubicle getting angrier with each step he takes. "It is always something with her we can never enjoy the moment, damn it." As he continued to talk to himself. "Do you know what the worst thing about all of this I'm is still fucking hungry I only ate two bites and my dumb ass threw it away.

Fats

Friday 16, 9:00 am Fats phone rings repeatedly.
"What's up?
"Shit smoking, what are you up too?"
"Trying to get some of that you are smoking."
"Bet, you know your cousin is over here."
"Well I knew his ass wasn't going to school. What his ass doing over there anyway?
"He in the bedroom with his girl Kayla."
Oh, cuz trying to get some let me find out."
"You haven't mess with him yet."
No, I was thinking about it though, but it is him and shorty first time I didn't want to mess it up for him."
"Yeah, I hear you but damn that I am on my way over there."
"Cool with me man." Deon hangs up the phone. Feeling higher than a kite. He thought, *where these girls get this shit. I could have done this another way, I might of have mess up a good thing up over there, damn. Oh well that is life you win some and you lose*

some. Deon finally gets up and walks out to his car. He opens the door and notices a blue bronco out the corner of his left eye. He turns and spots someone sitting in the driver seats. I swear Peaches better be in school. The driver notice him but turns his attention towards the front door. Where Peaches and some want to be Rastafarian looking dude walks out of the door. He starts walking towards them. As they were walking towards the truck, Peaches notice her brother. Deon was reading her lips as he was walking towards them.

"Oh, fuck my brother. Deon reads the dude lips.

"Who the fuck is your brother." Deon smiles as he gets to the guardrail.

"So, who your friend is?

"I am late for school I will talk to you later when I get home." Deon grabs her by the arm.

No, I think now is much better." She tries to whisper to Deon.

"Can you go away for a little while I am trying to do a little something and you are messing it up? I got this big brother I will call you later." Deon lets go of her arm, turns around, and starts to walk away. He stops when he hears Rasta talking trash.

"Yeah, she got this big bro or whoever the fuck you think you are. Take your yellow ass back to your car." He thought, *somehow, I'm going to regret this.* A big smile comes across his face, as he turns back around and notice his sister shaking her head with her hand over her face. She already knew old boy fuck up and it was time to pay the piper. The dude started talking more recklessly.

"This nigga must don't know who I am." As he gets closer to him, Deon tells him

"No, I don't know, so who you are, so tell me?" Rasta tries to swing on him yelling I am your worst— but Deon dodge it and hit him right into the ribs. Then grab his arm and hits him in the throat the dude drops to his knees on the ground grasping for air. Deon pulls his gun from behind him and starts pointing at the driver with it. He tells him do not make a move I know you are reaching. You do not want to do that. He yells why not. The driver looks up and see Deon is pointing at his sister with his other hand while still looking and pointing his gun at him. That is when he notice she had a 380mm pointing at his boy head. She begins to speak in a Jamaican accent.

"You really want to do this bomboclot"

It is 9:15 am and there is a knock at the door. Oh, that must be Deon. Fats open the door it is Black.

"What's up man?"

"Nothing, what's going on with you?"

"You know me, and something is always on."

"Come on in."

"You home by yourself, where is everybody?"

"You just miss D he is taking his girl up to the bus stop."

"Who Kayla they were up in here, let me find out my man hit that. That have to be the luckiest nigga I know."

"You didn't hear this from me, he ate that joint."

"Oh okay, what did he eat?"

"You know he ate that joint." Confusion was written all over Black's face.

"He ate it, Fats he ate what? He ate some weed?"

"Man are you slow and death. He ate the coochie man."

"Oh, he ate the coochie. "Right, now you get it."

"Stop playing Fats, you serious. Honestly I never knew anyone who have done it."

"Me either I only seen it getting done on a VHS."

"You know I am about to clown his ass, it's on and popping. Fats can I get some water?"

"Yeah, you know where the glasses are." Black gets up and walks into the kitchen. When there is another knock at the door. What is this, party central? Damion walks in.

It is 11:00 am and there is another knock at the door. Fats gets up to answers it.

"You know who it is."

"Man, where have you been?"

"Dealing with some bullshit."

"What it do Black?"

"Nothing what's up with you?"

"My crazy as sister got me out here about catch a case. Deon tells them both what happen.

"What happened to the two dudes?"

"Two cops were walking by and save their asses. I saw them coming around the corner before they saw me. I yelled cops to my sister, and we ran into my mother's house. The bama as nigga on the ground hop in the truck and drove off."

"You have this thing about trouble.

"What about it?"

"It follows you everywhere you go."

"Looks whose talking." Black interrupts them.

"Well fellas it was real, I will holla at you later, I have, a date with two big old bitties."

After Black exit the apartment, Deon ask about Damion.

"Where D at?"

"He's in the bathroom. He better not be taking a shit either. I need to tell you something though, but you didn't here this from me."

"Your cuz is out here eating."

"Okay, I hope he's eating good."

"Eating well is the correct form—Deon gives him a look.

"Umm like I was saying he's out here eating." More puzzle then before he ask.

"What is he eating? Fats nod his head slowly.

"Oh, he's out here eating. He flops down on the couch, behaving in a dysfunctional manner.

My cousin is out here eating booty. You sure he said he ate her out, went down on her, ate her pussy?" Fats look at him and slowly nods his head.

"Yes."

"Get the fuck out of here. You for real."

"Yes, he told me himself."

"Wow, what the fuck was he thinking, that's some nasty as shit. The kid cannot go out like that. Damn cuz that is some freak out shit." They both started laughing.

That boy always been weird I tell you.

"I know, he's has been in my bathroom a little too long. I'm just thinking about them two fools earlier. He started shaking his head my sister know better than this shit.

"You never bring that shit home an especially not to our mother house."

Leaving Work

3:00 pm and Lowell finds himself staring at the clock on the wall. Time is moving slow as hell today, when a female coworker who walks into his cubicle interrupts him.

"I see you are on the countdown. Lowell starts to smile.

"You know it I am ready to go home." How can you tell?

"You have the look, I can tell. I hear you though, so am I; it has been one of those days."

"Tell me about it, so what can I do for you."

"Well a group of us is going out for happy hour down the street. I wanted to invite you."

"Oh, really that sounds enticing, unfortunately I am going to have to pass. Thank you for thinking of me, I appreciate it."

"Okay if you change your mind, I am down the hall."

"Okay I will let you know if I change my mind. Penny right"

"Yes, it is." She flashes a beautiful smile. He smiles back.

"Not too bad at all." Still staring at the clock as soon as time hit 3:58 pm, Lowell jumps up it is time to go; he starts to pack up his belongings. When Mr. Matthews walks in his cubicle with another pile of folders. Awe where you are going home as he sits down in the chair in front of Lowell's desk. He begins to toss the folders on his desk. You need to postpone whatever you were planning to do tonight. He begins to lean back in the chair and put his shoes on Lowell desk. As Lowell looks at Mr. Matthews shoes with a slight grimace.

"Mr. Matthews you can get anyone to do this especially someone with less tenure then I."

"Mr. Reese. I don't want anyone else I want you boy."

"Boy." Mr. Matthews looks towards his side then behind him.

"Is there an echo in here?" Lowell shakes his head, then takes a second to gather himself. He thought, *this nigga do not know how dead he really is.*

Lowell sits down. While Mr. Matthews gets up, he tells Lowell to make sure he has the work done by tomorrow morning. He walks out of the cubicle laughing. Lowell was enraged he started throwing the folders across the room.

"Mother fucker!" He makes a phone call.

"I need some work put in." A voice answers.

"Name, time and the place."

"I will call you from another phone with the particulars." Lowell calls his girl and tries to apologize. After picking up the phone and answering it, she politely hangs it up on him, in the middle of his speech.

"Hello, hello he looks at the phone and hangs up. He gets up and walks down to his coworker Penny cubicle.

"Hey, you still going to happy hour?"

"Yes."

"I will meet you down there.

"That's good to me."

"I will see you later then."

"You can count on it." Once again, she flashes that beautiful smile of hers. Lowell walks back to the cubicle and picks the folders up off the floor. He calls Fats no one answered. He gets a call from his brother they started talking for a minute. After hanging up the phone. He thought, it's happy hour time.

Lowell walks up to the bar and see his coworkers drinking. He stops at the pay phone first to use it. Then joins them, I see all of you are having a good time. Penny started smiling when she sees him.

"You showed up."

"Yes, I am here to get my drink on."

"That is what I am talking about."

"What are you drinking?"

"An amaretto sweet and sour. Why are you looking at me like that?"

"Oh, nothing I see you are bringing out the big guns tonight." She starts laughing.

"Okay Mr. Funny man I am not a big drinker."

"So why come to a bar for happy hour then?"

"I guess to fit in; I am also new to the city. Besides how am I supposed to get to know everyone, especially you?" Lowell points to himself.

"Oh, you want to get to know me." Lowell ask the bartender for a double shot of tequila and another round for the young woman.

"Will that be a problem?"

"Will what be a problem?"

"Us getting to know each other?"

"I mean, it is kind of, up to you, I am in something right now and it is complicated. To be honest with you I don't know if I am coming or going."

"I see, well darling it is not as if I am asking for marriage or anything like that, I just want to get to know you."

"I hear you and that is not a problem, but I have a sneaky feeling as he points at her you are going to be trouble." She smiles,

"Who little owe me? Nah, I am just an innocent small town southern girl." She grabs Lowell shot glass from the bar and drinks it. Her face instantly becomes flustered with redness.

"I cannot breathe. Lowell tells her to take it slow take a deep breath as he puts his hand on her diaphragm. He conveys to her to take another deep breath as she fans her face with her hand.

"What in the hell was that?

"Well my dear that's what you call a double shot of tequila from Mexico." Lowell starts smile.

"You will be fine just have a seat and relax." She tries to sit in the barstool but misses it completely Lowell catches her in his arms before she hits the floor.

"My black knight in shining armor. I do declare." He helps her up and back to her seat. She starts to laugh hysterically.

"Wow, I feel good. I like the way this makes me feel." She looks around the bar.

Damn, why are my nipples so hard? She starts laughing again.

"Did I just say that aloud?" Which made Lowell laugh aloud.

"Hmm maybe that was a little too much for you." She grabs her amaretto and raise it up, to friends. She drank it to there was nothing left in her glass. She points to him and gesturing to come to her. He gets closer, she leans in, and they to begin kiss. Next thing they knew they were in the back of the bar in a corner kissing. She starts to unbutton her blouse.

"Tell me, do you want this?

"I do, but…and I cannot believe I am about to say this, because you are fine as hell. Yet we need to stop this."

"What, are you serious?"

"Unfortunately, yes, let me call you a cab. They started walking back to the bar.

"You're really a knight in shining armor. Thank you for not taking an advantage of me. She rubs his arm.

"We will talk about it on Monday." He goes over to the pay phone to call her a cab. After she gets into the cab.

"You are very sweet, thank you."

"Your welcome, have a goodnight. Lowell had a lot on his mind, he walks out of the bar to get some fresh air.

Redemption

It is early Saturday morning sometime after midnight and Lowell is in a state of distraught over the events that has transpired earlier that night. He calls his man Smurf who lives a few blocks away. Smurf was one of those people that always has his hand in everything trying to come up the best way he knew how. Always with some new type of business adventure.

"Hey, what's up man?"

"Money, I heard what happen to Fats man anything you need let me know."

"Thanks man I appreciate that."

"So, what's popping?"

"Just need to get my mind off a few things."

"I have just the right thing for you. How about you come over, I got you."

"That sounds like a plan I am on my way."

"See you when you get here my brother. He walks around to Smurf house he notices two big guys standing outside like you would see at a club.

"We need to pat you down sir."

"Are you serious what's going on in there?"

"If you want to see what's inside you need to be search, there is a cover charge but the boss wave it for you sir but not the search."

"Cover charge you two are funny. Okay let's do this." He raises his arms up, with a smirk on his face. Afterwards they open the door for him, and he walks inside. He looks around and is amazed. He sees his man Smurf, coming through a door.

"Damn nigga is it like that; you have a club up in here."

"You like it." He grins and spreads his arms apart. "Welcome to Smurfs."

"Damn, this is what I am talking about son. I thought you were just having your usual card game."

"I have that and them some the card games are upstairs the strippers are downstairs and you see what you see here. Strippers downstairs, what the hell."

"Strippers, I know where I will be from now on."

"Yes, strippers and an oasis of them. Alright then holla at me if you need anything, I need to take care of something."

"Okay dog holla at you later."

"Enjoy yourself tonight."

After walking around Lowell runs into some people he knew. Not in a mood for long conversation he heads upstairs to the poker tables. He takes a seat, but after losing a few bills, he decided to go back downstairs to the bar. He sat there for about fifteen minutes staring at his drink. That is when the bartender walks over and suggested to him how things work there.

"You ask me, your friendly but sexy bartender to make you, the customer a drink. I make such drink, a spectacular one mind you and pour it for you. Then you drink such drink and it is amazing. To the point it has you smiling and asking me what is in this, and may I have another one please. Then after that you pay for the, drink hopefully I get a very nice tip. See how that works, it is called cause and effect.

"He stares at the glass, so what is it called?"

"An Orgasmic Smile. He begins to smile."

"What is that is that, is that a smile bless his heart?"

"Okay you got me, hello my name is Lowell," as he reaches out to shake her hand.

"My name is Lolita glad to meet you."

"Lo and Lo, two cool nicknames what you think?"

"I like it."

She asks him. "Is everything okay? You look like you got a lot on your mind."

"More than you will ever know. Tell me something, what is a nice girl like you doing in a place like this?"

"She starts to laugh are you trying to hit on me with that old line."

"No, just asking I'm doing some soul searching. In your profession, I know you hear a lot of wild stories."

"True, you hear some real and some fake, but we all have heard them.

"So how do you know what's real and what's fake."

"Well to answer your question in layman's terms, we all wear a mask some different from others but still there is a mask. Some people wear them to hide their identity and then there are certain people who ware them to mask their feelings. Those who mask the nature of the beast inside them are very different." Lowell puts his glass down on the bar.

"The nature of the beast." "Hmm what does that mean?"

"Well, let us just say that sometimes a mask may conceal one's mind as a defense mechanism. "Shielding one from hurting him or herself or even others. There will always be people who ware mask seeking false power." "I guess devouring on the weak gives them some type invincibility."

"Sounds very interesting I guess I never look at it like that. What do you do besides bartend?"

"I'm a phycology major at George Mason why do you ask?"

"Just wondering I knew there was something different about you."

"How very perceptive of you, you're not just another cute face.

"Oh, so you think I'm cute."

"You are okay." Then she smiles.

"Just okay I hear you. Lowell turns around and starts to observe everyone interacting with one another. He sees a familiar face in the crowd this dude name Kenny. Who was neither friend nor foe? They were very close at one time, but you know how it is people change some for the better others for the worst. He was one of those type of dudes that grew up with you but never knew what they were thinking. One you always kept one eye open when you were around him. He'll be helping you out with his left hand. Yet would be robbing you with his right hand.

"Hey what's going on?" "What are you doing up in here man?"

"You know just chilling trying to relax".

"Man, I heard what happen to the big guy. "Are you okay?"

"Nah not really but I will be okay." "Let me know what's up you know I'm down for whatever man.

"That is good to hear bruh I appreciate that."

"I see you over here talking to the bartender she's nice man. Damn she have green eyes too." Lowell starts to laugh, yes, she does.

"Is that you man?"

"Nah, just conversing. So, what are you getting into Kenny?"

"Nothing just trying to get a few stacks, you know how it is out here."

"Yeah, I hear you Good luck with that." What really was on Lowell mind, was whom is this fool trying to rob up in here.

"I'm trying to celebrate man what are you drinking?"

"Thanks, but I'm okay I had enough already."

"Man come on I haven't seen you in about a month. "Man, I am trying to party. Hey bartender another round for my friend." Lowell stands up angrily.

"Nigga are you dumb as well as deaf I said I'm good why are you trying to be my best friend all the sudden. Nigga do you know something, trying to be all cozy up and shit. Man, just step."

"Aye Lo, it's not even like that."

"You still here. He looks him up and down. I said step off. I have enough shit on my mind."

"Damn man I was only trying to help."

"I don't need your help."

"If you want help someone go help the homeless, I'm sure they would love the help."

"I knew Fats before you, he was my friend too."

"Nigga, did you just say he was your friend? Some guys get between them. Lowell walks off, looking for a restroom, and ended up downstairs. Where he sat there in a chair looking depress, a young woman comes over.

"You want a lap dance baby?"

"No not now but maybe later." He just sat there depress looking at the dancers performing. The DJ starts to play Spread my Wings by Troop. He sees one of the servers walking by and stops her.

"Hey, can I get a bottle of water?"

"Yes, sir I will be right back with that." He thought to himself, *how did this happen.* She came back with a bottle of Evian water and a double shot of tequila.

"Where did this come from, I didn't order it?"

"It is compliments from the bartender."

"Okay thank you." He sat it on the table next to him. Today's events has taken their toll on him starting with Taylor and ending with his friends. He thought he might need to go the hospital. His attention was directed back towards the dancers again. Thirty minutes had passed by when he starts to look at his drink. He picks it up and thought, *this is for you Fats.* Candy by Cameo just finish playing, and the DJ tells the crowd that the girls are about to take a break for a little bit. We are going to slow it down just a little He starts playing Make it Like it Was, by Regina Belle. Lowell thought to himself, *I've been in here to long I need to take my ass home. I have to get up and go to the hospital in the morning.* He slowly tries to get up but falls back to his chair. That last one might have just been a tad bit too much he thought. Somebody Watching Me by Rockwell begins to play. Lowell starts to drink his bottle of water. He looks at the bottle, damn this drink tasted funny. Lowell tries to get back up but falls back in the seat. He begins to lose control over his body, shaking uncontrollable. He starts foam at the mouth. The exotic dancers started screaming that's when Kenny comes from behind a door and tries to save him. Come on man don't give up. He performs CPR on him don't died on me man come on. Meanwhile Smurf walk up to the bartender.

"You take care of that?"

"That is what you pay me the big bucks for boss." He looks at her and tells her to make that call. He hears the ambulance coming he tells one of his henchmen that is working with him to handle this. While he attends to a business matter upstairs. He tells his bartender to let him know what was said as he walks upstairs. Smurf and two of his bodyguards follows him to this room with a metal door at the end of the hallway. He walks in and there are three gentlemen sitting at a circle table with a man standing behind each of them.

"How may I help you?" One of them begin to speak.

"The question is not how you can help us but rather how we can help each other."

"Interesting." He said after rubbing his chin.

Meanwhile blocks away Damion is still up he cannot seem to fall asleep and is hungry as always. He wanted to get out of the house to get some fresh air. He walk outside still looking at the crime scene. He just sat there on the hard cold concrete. Contemplating what to do next. Numb to the cold as well as his harsh reality he continue sitting there thinking, about his family and friends. He briefly looks up and see Keisha light is still on. I started thinking, *why she is still up.* Shortly after he looks up again and see her standing in her hallway door. Softly she yells out to Damion.

"Come over here." He gets up and walks over to her.

"Are you okay?" she ask him, while hugging him.

"Yeah, I'm okay, I guess.

"I saw you out here by yourself. Why are you out here?"

"Just trying to clear my head."

"Its cold out here this should be the last place I would want to be. I know you're hurting. I wish I had the right words to say to you, but I don't."

"It's okay I don't think anyone right now would have the right words to say. It is what it is and there is no changing that. I mean it was bad enough my best friend is hurt and laid up in a hospital but my cousin too on the same damn night. What are the odds of that happening and I still don't know where Lowell is?

"Fats and I got into it. What if that was the last thing, we said to each other?" He leans against the wall looking dejected.

"It's okay if you want to cry." Damion pauses and gives her his undivided attention.

"Umm I am not going to cry I'm a man."

"Well it looks like the man was crying earlier."

"Come on Keisha not now."

"I apologize I am so sorry you are right this is not the time or the place. I guess we have been doing this for so long it comes naturally.

"I understand we have been going back and forth for years. Honestly, I do not want to keep doing that with you."

"Neither do me."

"Wait a minute did you just apologize are you okay let me check your forehead."

"Boy stop playing, I am not that bad. Your hands are warm though. A small smile appears on her face

"I do not know about that."

"Whatever." Then she pushes him.

I started smiling. "Why is that though?"

"Why is what?"

"Why have we been going back and forth for so many years?"

"Honestly, I don't know, it's has been like that since junior high school." I begin to take a step closer to her. "However, I would say this you always had my back.

"In addition, you always had mine. That is what friends are for." She leans in and kisses him on the cheek."

"What is that for?"

"For you being you." "Are you going to the hospital tomorrow?"

"Yeah you want to come with me?"

"Yes, if you don't mind."

"You know I don't I will call you in the morning."

"Okay you have a good night."

"You have a good night as well. Try to get some sleep okay."

"Okay I will. I watch her walk back to her apartment. I started walking back to my side of the front thinking shit I am still hungry when Keisha start yelling Damion's name. He turns around all nonchalantly with a smile on my face.

"What do you want now girl?" He sees her looking in the opposite direction. Where he see three people walking very fast towards my direction. With what appears to be shotguns. Oh, shit barely escapes as he takes off running towards his door. While trying to open the main door he notice through the door window that his front door was open. Within that second of a time frame, he thought, *did I just see someone just walk in.* Finally, in and down the steps, he slips and hits his head on the ground in front of his door. He hears the pump action of a shotgun. Where he sees his friends and him being fire upon like prey into pieces while sitting in the car. Unlike previously these rounds found their names. A voice emerges and ask him two questions and offered two answers.

What is a dream? A series of thoughts, images, and sensations occurring in a person's mind during sleep. What is a nightmare? A frightening or unpleasant dream. In this dream state Damion watches helplessly as time unfolds in reverse. From his grueling death, the death of his cousin as he went down fire his weapon. His best friend not even able to move in the driver seat to do anything except take most of the assault. He thought, *did Lowell make it?* As he laid there on that cold operating table dying. Time was steady flowing in the opposite direction. His family Kayla, Keisha, Darnell, Black, he was steadily reminiscing while hearing the doctors and nurses fighting to save his life. They were beginning to fade. The last thing he hears is a loud female scream and faintly call it. The time is 333 am Saturday, 17th. I'm too young, I don't want to die. His grandmother's words echoed in his ears. In life we rarely take a straight line to our destination. He thought to himself, *is this heaven or is this hell? Maybe it's neither, maybe it's…*

Well this story begins like any other typical story. The year was 1990. In addition, it was Damion, aka D was last ride at Eastern high school, and his plan was for him to go out unlike no other. It was Friday morning, and the sunlight gently crept across his sheets. When it reaches his face, he hears music playing in the background. It is his alarm clock going off. It is playing Mad World by Tears for Fears. He begins to yarn, and stretch, as he thought to himself: that is strange, I thought, *I left it on 95.5 FM. Must have been one of those badass sisters of mine playing with it again.*

He laid there snug up in his blankets and begins to reminisce about what happen to him the previous night. It started out a little crazy. However, it turned out to be better than expected. He pause for a second because he couldn't shake this feeling of familiarity when he begin thinking about it.

The End

www.ingramcontent.com/pod-product-compliance
Lightning Source LLC
Chambersburg PA
CBHW070630100726
47907CB00007B/1919